THE 'JUSTICE' QUINTET, BOOK FOUR

CLEAR TO KILL

Carey Harrison

CLEAR TO KILL

DR. CICERO BOOKS

www.carey-harrison.com
www.drcicerobooks.com

Dr. Cicero Books
New York Rio de Janeiro Paris
First Edition
Manufactured in the United States of América

ISBN: 0692742395
ISBN-13: 978-0692742396

The 'Justice' quintet consists of five separate, stand-alone books, connected only by theme: in each one a central character (or more than one) takes justice into his, or her, own hands. The previous books in the series are *Justice* (2013), *Who Was That Lady?* (2014) and *Dog's Mercury* (2015), all available from Dr. Cicero Books and from Amazon.com in both Kindle e-book and paperback editions.

For Firas and Samantha

On the ruins of what's to come
I stand
I'm the cursed Babylonian

From *Forgetting*
——F.S., translated by S.K.S.

Index of chapters

1. *The drop*

IT SEEMED TO ME THAT LIFE HAD ENTERED a phase of hell in which everything, fields, streets, even faces, partook of the same sad colours, like a photograph of a rainy day, and I wondered whether the world would ever recapture its brightness again.

Sometimes I think this was a prophetic thought, sometimes just a self-fulfilling prophecy. I may have studied too closely the colours of those times, until they lodged inside me, for life. I was young, I was 28 when they sent me to France for the third time, to pretend to belong, and to await confirmation of my orders.

WAITING IN THE rattling 'tortoise' to jump into the darkness that is France, I dwell as always in the sense that the fuselage of the Stirling is a uterus smoothed and emptied out by the multiple births that parachutists are, voided yet marked with shreds of skin——attached to the thin metal walls in the half-dark there are always nameless straps and cords swinging and banging against the sides, like the moorings of vanished predecessors——and I summon this sense and the desire to be free of this heaving groaning container so that the desire will weigh against the fear of the jump. Such fear as there is I can't really ascribe to the act of jumping, though. It's not the jumping, it's the thought of what comes after that puts the wind up you, while you're sitting there wondering what might be awaiting you. Babies must ask themselves the same question as they wait, squeezed half to death, in the birth canal. Where the hell are they sending me? Will there be a dark mushy field, or will I wind up spitted on a steeple like a morsel from the sky, or crash into trees or be greeted by searchlights and a hail of bullets? Will I be lit up like a fairground target? It's happened before.

Why is this life of ours so *grim*? Even to think this question feels like a betrayal. Years later when I read *1984* and picture Winston Smith scribbling in a diary in a corner where the thought police can't see him, I'm certain Orwell was tortured by the same feeling, the same question.

Because it's not just this tattered, quaking aeroplane that's grim, and not just the France below us that I picture monochrome and sad. Again the feeling comes, all too familiar, the one that belongs not only to this moment before a jump but increasingly to whole stretches of everyday existence. When I'm on a mission I prefer to think it's just a self-protective reflex, an enveloping membrane that seeks to tell me it's all right and that I'm not really about to fling myself into space and into mortal danger even if I land safely, but it's clearly nothing to do with the drop, since it now recurs in times and places quite without imminent danger or threat of any kind. The feeling is one of estrangement. The thought that comes with it is that this life is simply an episode, an interval of punishment, presumably for sins committed in a previous life (though it's a poor system when the condemned man can't even recall his crime); and when I say 'this life' feels like an episode I mean this particular life with my curious origins and childhood that sets me apart, and this life that contains a particular London and a lumbering Stirling bomber and a jump into a France that seems in my mind to have turned into a region of hell.

Hello, future, I want to say to our heirs, to generations yet unborn. We are your parents. This is what gave rise to you. This, this dark grey rainy hell on the outside and this gloomy remoteness on the inside: this is what you come from.

ALL SUCH THOUGHTS and feelings vanish in the whipping noise and terror of the jump. The goggles are no better than last time, and the wind searing my face is as good a guide to the proximity of France as anything my eyes can manage, while I fall spreadeagled. But what's to see, anyway, until I pull the ripcord and await the sensation as the chute opens and seems to pull my torso from my body in a vicious wrenching halt that might just as well be me hitting the ground? But isn't.

But isn't, as I dangle in the darkness.

2. *Mother*`

I NEVER KNEW MY FATHER. I ALWAYS SAY this in a modest tone——I will usually have already planted the information that my father died in the First War——that serves to evoke images in my listener's mind: the telegram at the door and the babe-in-arms unable to comprehend his mother's tears. In fact I simply never knew my father. I never had any idea who he was, and my mother took the secret to her grave. Quite possibly she herself didn't know.

How did you get into this game? When the invariable question comes from a new colleague, I reply, "I was born an SOE operative." This usually amuses them, because they know exactly what I mean. No-one joins our game unless they were born to it. I know it sounds unhealthy, to put it mildly, but the Special Operations Executive is our mother and our father. You either understand what I'm talking about or you don't. To put it as plainly as I can, there's nothing you can experience or learn from others that could turn a life of unremitting, solitary danger into a compulsion, unless it answers to something in your soul.

I had a person I thought was my father, until I was twelve years old. It was the happiest day of my childhood when I found that Albert Ferris wasn't my father, but only my Aunt Sara's boyfriend. Not even an uncle. Not even an uncle by marriage. No relation at all. He was a big bald man with bulging eyes, he had hair sprouting from several orifices and from every crevice of his body, and the fancy suits he wore never succeeded in making him any less of a gorilla. I took against his smell when I was little, and not all the cologne in the world had been able to get it out of my nostrils. Thinking that Albert was my father, I watched my growing body with anxiety and suspicion, waiting for it to sprout the mat of trademark Ferris hair. (I've always had unusually thick eyebrows, and this had me worried from the beginning, expecting the rest of my body to follow suit.) It was only when I learnt that I had not a single gene in common with Albert that I was able to relax about my physical future, for the first time in my life, and wait to see who and what I was.

I was sorry, though, to learn that Aunt Sara wasn't my mother, as I had hitherto believed. Edie, my real mother, had given me to her sister when I was a few weeks old. Sara wanted a child, Edie didn't. It was as simple as that, they both told me, especially since my father wasn't around to object. It was 1915, and for all I know it's true that my father, as I tell people, never came back from the war.

Of the two sisters, Sara was a slightly more maternal sort of person than Edie was, although that isn't saying much. In fact it wasn't Edie's idea at all that she would get me back when I was twelve, and that I would be told the truth about which of the sisters was my real mother.

It was my stepfather Harry's idea, when he found out that Edie had a kid, namely myself. At the time Sara and Albert Ferris were on the outs, and it seemed likely that I might want for a father, or at least a father figure, if Albert and Sara broke up, as in the end they did. Harry said the boy should get to know his real mother and that we could all live together, Harry, Edie and myself, in North London, where Harry's furniture business was. I think he was hoping to show Edie what a good father he would be if they had a child together. Harry was well-meaning but, to be frank, a fool. He really thought Edie's reservations about having a child with him were because she wasn't sure what kind of a father he would make. She just never wanted children ever.

But to go back a bit: I was raised in the rowdy, smoky, glorious district of Montparnasse, in Paris (I'll explain why) by Sara and Albert Ferris, if you could use the word 'raised' for Albert's contribution. Sara was a London showgirl, she was originally from Basildon in Essex, which was where she and Edie grew up. Rawlinson was the family name, and it was the name I took when I spat the word Ferris off the end of my name and out of my life and came back to London to live with Edie and Harry in Finsbury Park. I became Alan Rawlinson.

I suppose it's a bit of a euphemism to say that Aunt Sara, my surrogate mother, was a showgirl, although that was what we always did say. The world that she and Edie frequented was devoted as much to entertaining men in whatever manner they would pay for than it was to dancing. The Rawlinson girls must have been a pair of honeys, in their prime. Sara big-nosed and blonde, not the cornsilk blonde of the movies but a coarser, more robust kind, and Edie dark and a lot silkier, with the profile of a hawk. Both tall. Both of them taller than I am, which argues either poor nutrition or the likelihood that I take after my unidentified Dad. In his absence, I am the runt of the family. Runt Rawlinson, that's me.

Sara had a doomed instinct for rotten men (in that regard Edie was smarter), and wound up with Albert Ferris, who was the manager of a West London "pally" or palais de danse when the war ended. He took a dance troupe to Paris, not an uncommon venture in the wake of the war, for what was supposed to be a month's work. A lot of Brits had become familiar with the dives of

Montparnasse. Even the Folies Bergères line-up was full of London tarts. The girls would pretend to be French while they were dancing, and let out cries of Ooh la la. Off the stage they were a bit of a disappointment to punters from across the Channel, but then they'd have a good laugh and a cuddle and a *So where are you from, then?* and they were set. Albert and the girls, including Aunt Sara, found a niche at a place called the Mon Chat Noir (if you're as old as sin and you went there between the wars you likely caught a glimpse of Sara), and they never went back to Hammersmith.

Eventually Aunt Sara did return to London, ten years later, when her dancing days and her Albert Ferris days both came to an end. By that time they'd been shouting and screaming at each other for a while, and throwing crockery in the approved French manner, and my soon-to-be-stepfather Harry had rescued me from this crazy Paris household full of Mon Chat Noir girls coming and going and occupying Albert Ferris's bed when Sara wasn't looking. Sadly, when Sara came back to London, she fell ill. She was much too young to have cancer, everyone said, but I doubt if cancer has much respect for age. It was a capillary cancer, Edie told me, and because of the sound of the word I've always imagined it as a kind of fatal caterpillar that crawled out of Sara's womb, where Edie said the illness started, and then trailed its way across other organs. Because it didn't occupy the organs but only coated them, Edie said, you couldn't get rid of it. Sara suffered all through the war, only to die the week before the Normandy landings. I always felt that even though her condition got steadily worse as the war went on, she got progressively less attention, what with the casualties of the Blitz filling up the hospitals and everyone having lost someone or had their life blighted in one way or another.

I always tried to think of Aunt Sara as she had been in the apartment off the Place Pigalle, funny and salty and always with a saucy comeback when Albert started riding her. In one way I was glad to be away from the shouting and screaming, when Harry took me back to London. In another way I missed my lovely wild and grimy Montparnasse where nobody much noticed where I was and when I came and went, in those last couple of years when Sara and Albert were at war. By the age of ten I'd found myself a backstage niche at the Mon Chat Noir, helping Madame Pelletier, a seamstress who came in to do repair work on the girls' outfits, which tended to burst a seam or two under the pressures of the can-can or the customers (more often the latter). She was getting on, Mme P., or so I thought then, though she probably wasn't much more than 40, and she hated having to stop the sewing machine to adjust the material she was working on, letting the treadle click on, winding down, clip-clopping on like an obedient but ignorant dog on a leash, who senses that his mistress has stopped to look in a *vitrine*. My job was to feed the clothing into the machine for her, and I loved it. I loved handling the chiffon and the voile, and I loved being backstage during the day when the nighttime smells were still held in the dressing-rooms along with the last of the cigarette smoke, like haze in a retort. Madame would slip me a few sous at the end and I'd be up the stairs and out into the Place Pigalle like a bank robber, running through the pavement crowds in search of my mates. I was a child of the street, with plenty of friends like myself. In London, with Harry and Edie, I was suddenly accountable again, and couldn't just walk out the door and come home when I pleased. Edie might have let me do it, but not Harry.

I've wondered from time to time why Edie ever mentioned my existence to him. Did she think that if she married Harry and then one day Sara told him the truth he'd be furious and throw her out? He hated to be lied to. But she could weather rows, could Edie, just like her sister. That Basildon household they came from must have been a whirlwind, a howling storm. Perhaps that was why neither of them was crazy about having kids——by which I mean perhaps it was their own childhood they didn't want to be reminded of.

So, to return to Harry Seltzer and his discovery of me, I dare say Edie may have owned up to Harry that she'd had a child so as to try and get it across to him that she didn't want or need to do it again. Being Harry, he didn't get the message. He came to Paris and brought me back to London, after telling Albert Ferris what he'd to do him if Albert laid a hand on Harry's girlfriend's sister again. As much of a fool and an innocent as Harry Seltzer was, he was big, even bigger than Albert, and he packed a punch.

He was well off, too. Edie had landed in the butter when she caught Harry's eye. Which is why she put up with the return of the prodigal, her young 12-year-old son whom she'd hardly laid eyes on more than four or five times in her life, and who could hardly fail to notice that where Sara actually liked kids, his "real" mother had to pretend to care for her own son. To be fair to Edie, she had quite a lot to put up with from me, maybe more than she expected. Her kid was to all intents and purposes a little French boy, a ruffian dragged up in the Paris gutters since he was three. All I knew was to pick a fight and how to take a punch to the gut. I'd been to school——which was where most of the fighting took place——but whatever I'd learned there was in French, and gutter French at that.

I must have been as out of place in Finsbury Park as a panther on a leash.

Harry sent me to the Merchant Taylors' school, at his expense. It still makes me shake my head, to think about him taking a long calm look at me and sending this scrawny, combative little Paris urchin off to public school instead of parking me somewhere that suited my manners. And although it took a good few years, blow me if I didn't come out sounding like a public schoolboy. Not quite Eton and Harrow, but I could impersonate a toff pretty well.

That was on the outside, the part that six years of British schooling had polished up. Who on earth I thought I was when I was 18, inside, under the middle class veneer, I've no idea. Harry Seltzer sized me up once more and sent me off to Woolwich, to the Shop, as it was known, the old Royal Military Academy (this was before it was amalgamated with the RMC at Sandhurst), to combine my respectable vowels and my street fighting instincts. It must have worked for me for a time, because I thrived.

Unfortunately I'd always had a criminal tendency, acquired in Paris when thieving was the game my schoolfriends all went in for and I had to be the best and the most daring. I was an addict, though I didn't realize it, by the time I came back to London with Harry. I simply never got caught at Merchant Taylors, where I preyed on the other boys in a mindless sort of way, not for the small sums of money I stole——Harry never kept me short of pocket-money——but for the pleasure of it.

Partly, it was about not getting caught, but mainly it was to have a life of my own that no-one could share. For many people I dare say that's the opposite of what they want; they're longing for someone with whom they can share everything. When I looked round the SOE canteen, we were an odd-looking, various lot but we did have one attribute in common: sharing was not our thing. Try asking one of us for a taste of our shepherd's pie.

At Merchant Taylors I was just keeping in practice at being myself. I used to imagine it was Alain, my little Parisian self, who stole, and who was the real me underneath, that no-one knew. They couldn't see Alain when they looked at me, although he was looking back at them, and they couldn't see him when he slipped down empty corridors and into someone's temporarily vacated rooms.

Alain was the Invisible Man. I didn't think of him as French, especially. He was an older, deeper form of me. It was just that I'd got into the habit of shoplifting in Paris, and of picking the occasional Parisian pocket because that's where I was and that's what my pals did. And good old Alain went on doing it until I was caught red-handed at the Shop and revealed myself to be not at all the sort of person an officer in training and a gentleman should be.

They threw me out on my ear.

Edie screamed the house down, and Harry was quietly furious and made me work at one and sixpence an hour in one of his furniture showrooms until I paid back the forty pounds I was found to have stolen. Fifteen months it took me.

And all the time Reggie Peterson was watching me. Watching to see if I would stay the course, working for Harry. Watching, knowing what I'd done at Woolwich, and waiting to see if I was the kind of chap he thought I was.

3. *Reggie*

CUP OF TEA IN THE BACK ROOM AT MAUDIE'S
tea-house in Wigmore Street. *Maudie's* was all it said on the
outside. It was a genuine tea shop. Few of the regulars
there even knew there was a back room. But that's where
it all started, for almost all of us. Cup of tea and a chat.
Better than an interview in an office, if only because the
candidate would be a little less on his or her guard.

"Had tea with Uncle Reggie?" was the question many
baffled soldiers were asked by their superior officer, from
'41 onwards. It was the codeword, or code-phrase, and if
you knew what it meant you'd already been vetted by
Special Operations to see if you were MCR material, as we
called it. We were Middle Class Ruffians. The middle class
affiliation was the class bond that our masters believed in
as a badge of trust, as the only thing that kept us together,
since being ruffians we were therefore natural renegades. It
wasn't just that we talked the same way. Public school was
a club we'd belonged to and would always belong to.
Working class ruffians might at some point mutter, "Sod
the lot of you," and decide to serve their own interests
instead of Uncle's. MCRs wouldn't betray the club. What
would be left for them in life if they did? Working class
ruffians would win the war, we liked to think, with dirty
deeds on the front lines. Our job was different. It was to
fillet the enemy behind his own lines, with skulduggery.

Of course I didn't see myself as an MCR at all.
Perhaps lots of others in Special Operations didn't either,
for whatever reason. I was still Alain, under the veneer of

my vowels, I could take a punch in the gut from Gérard and trade one to the head. I'm a spy from the streets, I thought. Runt Rawlinson, *c'est moi*.

I came in on the ground floor in 1940, during the first few months of SOE, long before Churchill gave us the green light to go into France and mix it up. As I say, Uncle Reggie (whose name wasn't Reggie) had already pricked me out as one of those soldiers he was after, "useless in peace, irreplaceable in war," as he put it: dogged, insubordinate ("bloody-minded" was Reggie's word), and utterly committed to leading a double life.

I'd been toiling in the Finsbury Park showrooms for three years, four and a bit if you count the time I spent carting the furniture in and out of the warehouse while paying off my Woolwich debt, when Reggie himself came in, saying he was looking for a nice desk. All I saw was a plump fellow in a suit, with a face like Billy Bunter in the comics, red-cheeked and jovial. He looked like every other fat man you'd ever seen, and if his French hadn't been so bloody awful he'd have made a brilliant agent himself in his nerveless, bland and cheerful way.

"A desk, sir?" I asked.

"I mean the sort of desk a chap could sit at and look important without really trying." Reggie said. "What have you got in that line?"

"Nothing really, sir," I said, a little puzzled because this fat bloke in a suit could see at a glance that Harry's stock in trade was unpretentious three piece suites and other cheap suburban décor, nothing fancy.

"You don't look like the sort of fellow who'd know much about sitting on his backside for a living," Reggie said. "Where are you heading with this lark? Fancy selling furniture all your life?"

I'd no idea what he was getting at, but there was a twinkle in his eye that stopped me from getting smart with him.

"Merchant Taylors School, '28 to '34," he went on without a change of tone, "then RMA till you were given the boot for conduct unbecoming in '36. Have I got the right chap?"

"Who are you?" I said.

"I'm your Uncle Reggie."

"Haven't got an Uncle Reggie." This was something that others might have said with more confidence than me. I could have had two Uncle Reggies and never known about it.

"Have now, my son. If you want one. We're looking for fellows with a taste for adventure, military style, but not too military, if you catch my drift. Officially sanctioned, but not official. On nobody's books but our own. And we don't keep books."

He could have been singing my personal national anthem. I dare say he knew it.

"We look after our own, because no-one else will. But don't be too excited, boyo. This is nasty all the way through. That may be your idea of fun, but we don't want anyone so reckless they'll take others over the edge with them. So take your time and think about it. We need people who can hold their water."

He said some other stuff about friendship and how what he had to offer was the wrong place to look for it, because you soon learned not to make friends with those who were probably about to die. I was barely listening. I knew that for better or for worse my number had just come up.

Then he was inviting me to tea with someone called Maudie, I thought, at number 14, Wigmore Street, but I was already looking deep into the back of his sparkling yet strangely dead eyes to try and learn something at last, anything at all, about my kind.

4. *Vive le runt*

WHAT IF THERE HAD NEVER BEEN A WAR, and never been a Special Operations unit? What would have become of Runt Rawlinson? I can't believe I'd have spent my life as a salesman in Harry Seltzer's furniture showrooms and wound up (as Harry junior has——of whom more shortly) turning into the heir Harry wanted. I'd be a jailbird now. A jailbird or a millionaire or the thing I later was for an all-too-brief moment, a fashionable party-giver introducing girls to upper crust delinquents. Pandar by appointment to His Lordship. I could have been another Stephen Ward. My life's been filled with Christine Keelers and Mandy Rice-Davieses, both of whom I knew to say hello to and pat their sweet flesh in passing. Tarts and showgirls——let's face it, I have Sara and Albert to blame for this, and Montparnasse——are in my blood and in my heart. They raised me, the girls of the Mon Chat Noir.

Has anyone been as sexy, ever in my life, as Trudy, whom I'd known since I was four and who still sat me on her lap when I was a randy little eight-year-old (trust me, eight-year-olds can be randy), and who finally, on my twelfth birthday, introduced me to the mysteries? Who could match Trudy, who was blonde and pale with a face as round and flat as a saucer, and huge blue eyes and the softest, most fragrant body in the world? All my life I've been searching for someone that could hold a candle to her, knowing perfectly well that what I'm searching for isn't Trudy but my twelve-year-old self. I might as well be searching for a live pterodactyl.

But never mind the girls, for the time being. It's July 1940, France has fallen, and Uncle Reggie has arrived just in time to save my life.

One brush with the regular military had put me off for good (even assuming they'd've had me back, with my record), but I'd rather have topped myself than spend the war touting sofas in North London. I didn't have the patience to be a salesman, and of course everyone wanted to know, even if they didn't say it aloud, why a small but apparently intact male in his late twenties wasn't placing himself at the service of his country. I quickly got sick of that. By early 1940 Harry Seltzer was ready to see me go, too, despite having guided my life so carefully towards a future in furniture. (He never did think I'd make a soldier, but he believed the Shop would turn me into a tidier human being, and he was right about that. I've been known for neatness ever since.) It wasn't my lack of enthusiasm for sofas that eventually convinced Harry to cut me loose. What happened was that Edie got pregnant again at the age of 43, to her horror and Harry's delight, after a gap of 24 years. I can still see the smile on Harry's face——in my mind he's always there in that one instant, a gleaming Harry pushing open the glass entrance door and striding into the showroom to bring me the news.

This lets me off the leash (lets Alain the panther off the leash, anyway) at last, and little Harold junior, who could have been my kid rather than my baby brother, given his age, takes up all their attention from then on. Instead of clucking over Alan's lost opportunities they cluck over little Harold's baby steps. Perfect, as far as I'm concerned.

At first sight the folks in the back room at *Maudie's* don't seem like a convocation of the damned. I decide——not entirely mistakenly——that it's we, not they, who are required to be damned. We, the willing tools. The executive branch, who will be sending us to our doom, or at least onto the chopping block with a good chance of never coming back, can be ordinary suffering humans with a heart and a troubled conscience. (I exempt Uncle Reggie, who had neither.)

Netta, neat features and neat dark hair, certainly seemed like such a person, over a cup of tea, and I was startled to find when I got the thumbs-up and joined the fledgling organisation that she was in charge of training field operatives. I'd assumed that she would be the house matron, applying kind words and poultices. At first encounter it was all very public school, and I'd say anyone would probably have passed the test who'd been through that system and knew the right mixture of deference and cheek with which to treat the beaks. Reggie himself, still gleaming and preening as if he'd learned his whole act from Charles Laughton in the movies, was the only one of the high-ups on the interviewing committee who gave off any sense of ever having been in a fight and had his nose bloodied. He was my man, from the beginning. Besides, he'd picked me out himself.

He knew much more about me than my school and military track record and of course my French upbringing, although without these (above all the French upbringing) he wouldn't have been interested in me at all. Reggie knew about Aunt Sara and Albert Ferris. He'd even spoken with my old friend Gérard, punch-in-the-gut Gérard, whom I'd only seen once since I was a teenager. Gérard had visited me in London when we were twenty or so and he was still no more than an overgrown *voyou* without a job and I was a budding artillery officer, thank you very much. After that weekend we lost track of each other in a hurry. But Uncle Reggie found him. I always had a dark feeling that he knew about every single person in my life, even Trudy, who Aunt Sara said had retired to Eastbourne, although I'd made enquiries there myself without success. He may even have known who my real father was. If anyone did, it would have been Reggie.

By temperament, he was a collector. That's a human type, and I dare say you're born to it as much as you're born to being a field operative. I've always envied the collector type. Your calling keeps you busy all the time, without intervals to think about who you are and what you're doing.

5. *The epitome of shag*

UNDER NETTA'S WATCHFUL EYE, THE chap in command of unarmed combat training was a fellow we called Julian Wilson (another *nom de guerre*), who also gave us weapons training until we got someone who actually believed in weapons training for field operatives, which Julian didn't. Well, he believed in knives, but his argument was that you couldn't meaningfully train to use a pistol at close range since this was as much a matter of luck and opportunity as it was of marksmanship, and that field operatives wouldn't be carrying rifles or any longer range ordnance. This line of thinking quickly went by the board as we became more professionalized and our bureaucrats commissioned special weapons and required of us all manner of skills, some of them daft, ranging from cryptography to animal spoor identification. No doubt the idea, as with the collector mentality, was to keep us busy between missions.

Julian's real motive for despising weapons was that he had no patience, as he admitted himself, with the business of dismantling the things. Of course if you love firearms you love to dismantle them, so I dare say that indifference and not impatience lay at the root of Julian's attitude to weapons training. What he loved was to step in close, go man-on-man and bend and twist and exert mastery over another body, before disabling him or cutting his throat. No doubt there was a sexual element to this pleasure in locking another body to your will. Despite rumours to the contrary, 'J,' to use his nickname——you had to acquire a nickname even if you were already wearing a pseudonym——was an inveterate womaniser, to our knowledge. He'd also been a champion wrestler. In infancy it had been his way of blowing off steam, as it is for many kids, but, as he said, he'd never stopped. According to 'J', if everyone could just have a good wrestle every morning they'd be relaxed for the rest of the day. It brought you into touch with your body. Then you could be as *shag*, as lazy and casual, as you liked. *Shag* was a word 'J' brought us from his Harrow schooldays. When he wasn't engaged in sports or unarmed combat, 'J' was the epitome of *shag*.

It became my ambition too. I hadn't been a wrestler but as small as I was I'd been a brawler all my life, and 'J' recognized me, as Uncle Reggie had, as one of his own. I loved the training, even the learning by rote and the classroom hours, the cissy stuff as 'J' called it, full of arcane, half-baked instruction about potions and poisons and the bacteria we were going to slip into the water supply on Hitler's private train. 'F' section, F for France, was my home, and in my heart it still is.

It was a bit like being privately tutored, in a uniform, with a few select pals (rather a lot of pals as time went by). Aside from the hand-to-hand specialists, experts arrived to train us including a professional actor who taught the art of disguise, plus various old espionage hands to teach tracking and avoiding being tracked, codes and cyphers, and my favorites, burglary and sabotage. A *bona fide* ex-con, Derek Carter, showed us the miracles you could achieve with a bent pin and a protractor, or if needs be any old piece of plastic. Map reading and compass work we practised up in Inverness, in the worst possible conditions. This soon sorted the good 'uns from the rest. I know this sounds implausible from someone who faced death at German hands, over and over, but not much in life compares to a swarm of Highlands midges, when roused.

Later on the powers that be brought in all kinds of psychological tests and assessments, but I still thought an Invernesshire bog in the middle of the night was the best guide to natural aptitude.

As the war went on we also acquired a lot of crackpot gadgets, mostly killing devices, which I personally had little time for. Making gizmos kept the boffins busy, but never saved anyone's life in the field so far as I know. Quick thinking was what you needed, not a fountain pen with a dart in it.

The most useful stuff came from the detonations experts, much of which I was able to use in the field, on my second mission, when my team blew up the railway lines around Toulouse, and disabled locomotives far more effectively than any airborne attack. We also put paid to a great many bridges across the Tarn and the Garonne, which was work that gave me childish pleasure. Even now I can hardly see a bridge, or for that matter a train without starting to think about how best to blow it up using the minimum of explosive.

I had a natural feel for destruction, Reggie said. My work in the Tarn-et-Garonne had shown as much. This was just as well, because my previous mission had been at best a mixed success. Its purpose had been the formation of a new *réseau* or so-called circuit, a local resistance network, which required me to liaise with the French *maquis* in the region of the Landes, and work with people I didn't trust any more than I did the Air Pen with its stupid dart. Time proved me right in many individual cases, but until the Tarn all my first sortie seemed to prove, to Uncle Reggie and the rest, was that diplomacy wasn't my long suit, and that I wasn't brilliant at recruitment either. I could have told them that.

From then on I saw more action. In Toulouse I was able to link up with other SOE people and steer clear of the double agents with whom the local resistance groups were riddled. It was SOE or no-one as far as I was concerned, and I never regretted it. I'd like to say I never lost sight of Uncle Reggie's original warning about the perils of forming close friendships with men and women who might be dead the next day, but when you're working alongside people who're putting their life on the line, and when they do their job through thick and thin, you can't help surrendering a part of yourself to them, without even knowing it. To say you trust them doesn't describe it, at least until you learn what the word 'trust' really means. I came to think of love itself as a sub-department of trust. Trust someone with your life and, if that isn't love, then what's love but a fool's paradise, a holiday from reality? Even now if I meet or hear of someone who was in the SOE, whom I never met because they served in Albania or Greece, or Italy, or Crete, it brings me close to tears.

And it takes me back to the many places, Guildford in the early days and then Beaulieu and beautiful Arisaig in the Highlands, where I felt for the first time that I lived with others in mutual respect. I've said that SOE was a continuation of public school (and of the Royal Military Academy too, which was also full of chancers and skyvers who would be sorted out, their parents hoped, by the RMA), with its clubby nonchalance hiding a ruthless eye for winners and losers, but in another sense it was like a public school turned on its head. You could carve out your own niche regardless of name or money, or family connections. No easy pickings here for the mummy's boys from good homes who made up the officer caste at public and military school; here it was the bad eggs and the loners who graduated top of the class. Some of our best-groomed daredevils began sweating and babbling as soon as they reached enemy territory and were arrested in occupied Europe by the first German they saw; others, hopelessly shag, and subsequently doomed to a peacetime career——if they survived——of loafing around their local town until the pubs opened, were inspired and nerveless wartime agents, able to talk their way out of any trouble because they never took any of it too seriously in the first place. 'Duffle' Ponting, known by his one piece of winter attire and also as 'Toodle-pip' after his favourite expression, had already escaped twice from German custody, the second time with stolen German papers, when he found himself conducting a long intricate conversation in German with an officer from the *Abwehr*, in the corridor of a train in Normandy, and was able to relax so completely that at the end of it he forgot to say *auf wiedersehen*. Turning to go, he came out with "Toodle-pip!" instead. Poor Duffle told this story himself to our colleague Teapot Armfield, in Buchenwald concentration camp, where they both wound up, but from which, unlike several of his fellow-agents including the celebrated Armfield, Toodle-pip never emerged.

In other words, when you went into the field you discovered who you were, as a field operative. No amount of training gave you so much as a hint. You could have all the unarmed training skills of a karate black belt, you could know everything about how to shape a charge and how to detonate gelignite in adverse weather, you could be a virtuoso at operating one of our ghastly two-way radios that weighed 45 pounds in its backpack and drowned several of our men who touched down in marshland, you could know the codebook back to front, but if you froze up when you heard the word, "*Papiere!*" or turned a corner slap into a platoon of German soldiers, you were doomed.

I can't blame 'J' or Netta and her team of instructors. They did their best to put us under pressure. They locked us up and grilled us, starved us under blazing light day after day to see if we could withstand interrogation, but we still knew at the back of our mind that they weren't going to kill us. "It'll be different when you're out there," they kept saying, "with forged documents and without a friend in the world." Well, it was different. But that wasn't the heart of it. *You* were different.

Everything was finally in play, *rien ne va plus*, the roulette wheel was spinning and it really was your life on the line and nobody would care for long if you turned and ran and died face down in a ditch with a bullet in your back. It was time to face the music. See what you were made of.

Because I survived a number of scrapes, I was sometimes mentioned in the same breath as "Lucky" Lecky Thurgo, the paladin of St Nazaire and other jaunts. In time, "Runt" became a badge of prowess; between missions (and after the close shave I had in the Tarn, when my radio was traced and on the way to Gestapo headquarters I managed to bribe my captors, two French policemen who believed I was French, into letting me go), I served as an instructor for a while, and I could sense people pointing me out and whispering, "hero." I had my pick of the typing pool and didn't neglect to take advantage. Anyone who came back from occupied Europe twice or more times was like a talisman, and I liked being a talisman. In professional and social life I kept aloof, but that was part of the act. Between four walls I was ready to be rubbed, any time.

I like to think I never fell for my own fame, all the same. The odds lengthened against your coming back a third time, if you started to believe your own legend. And the odds were long enough already. Caution was fifty percent of it, Teapot used to say, and the other fifty percent was luck. You could be as cool as Bulldog Drummond in the comics, and it wouldn't save you unless Providence was on your side.

I knew I had something, though. Everyone knew it. People who kept coming back had something. Not just luck——everyone knew that "Lucky" Thurgo's nickname derived from his given name, Alec, or Lecky, and not from good fortune alone——but you needed something forged in your stars as surely as it was in your temperament. When things went wrong in the field, as they continually did, when the police showed up at the rendez-vous instead of your contact, when your bolt-hole was raided and the back door blazed with torchlight, or when you glanced from the window of your compartment to see Gestapo climbing purposefully aboard at both ends of the train, you either froze or you came alive. I always felt the same astonishing reaction. Time slowed down. Whatever was now to be done, including sifting through the options, there was more than enough time to figure out the best course, settle for it in your heart, and proceed calmly. Calmly, knowing that you'd had all the time in the world, that you'd studied the situation and made the best and only choice.

It was a strange sensation, one of being doubly alive. I was alive in the moment, living it in all its fear, and alive in another sense which was like pure electricity, the excitement precisely of being in danger and knowing it and living it to the full. You might make the wrong choice but you made it knowingly, seeing the moves ahead like a game, one throw of the dice after another in a kind of ecstasy——a kind of sickness, you might call it——of presence. Sometimes I thought I was already dead, I thought I was seeing my actions in retrospect and that my death awaited and that I was allowed to be gloriously alive because these were my final instants. As indeed they might have been, on more than one occasion.

I remember talking to Sergeant-Major Mills, V.C., who kicked down the door of a barracks full of sleeping German soldiers, early one morning in northern France after the D-Day landings, and killed the entire barracks-full with a single drum of his Thompson, shooting them like rats in a basement (those were his own words), on and on until every one of the fleeing men was dead and the empty drum spun on in the silence. He walked out into the early morning light——it was June, and seemed like bright day, he said, at four a.m.——and paused briefly to clean his steel-rimmed spectacles. Then he walked over to the adjoining barracks, a hundred yards away, where, as strange as it may seem, not a single man had stirred from sleep. There he again kicked the door down, and with his second clip killed every single soldier in the barracks, as before. That done, he emerged completely unscathed and with just over one hundred and fifty enemy dead to his credit. How in God's name did he feel, I asked, when he emerged onto the little parade ground with two single-handed massacres behind him?

"Blest," he said. "If you really want to know, Runt. Humbled. I wondered if there was anything in the world I couldn't do, that day. I also felt——and I don't usually tell this part," he said, "only I know you've seen enough action yourself to recognize what I'm saying——I also felt as if some part of me had gone, possibly forever. For the first time in my life I was quite ready to die, I mean to die that very day, although I never had the opportunity. I felt as if I'd been allowed to become a pure extension of my training. Of my weapon, if you like. I didn't think I'd ever get all of me back again."

He took off his glasses and stroked the bridge of his nose, before re-installing the glasses.

"And I didn't. I didn't really." He looked up, peering at me know to see if I understood. "Part of me simply died along with the rest of them, those soldiers. I think you have to accept that, in war. You don't survive, even if you come back alive. Part of you doesn't."

There had been plenty of pieces written about Mills, and even a book devoted to his exploits, but something prevented him from becoming one of the better-known heroes of the war. I suspected, though I didn't care to ask Mills if he shared my view, that this was because his crowning achievement, the reason for his medal and his fame, was unadulterated carnage. It had taken guts to step into the first barracks, and even more to step into the second one, where he might have been walking into a hail of gunfire, but in a sense it had been, as Mills said himself, like shooting rats in a basement. The numbers he killed were the thing that would forever be associated with his name. Nonetheless, he had reached a pinnacle. I couldn't help feeling that he had received less than his due, as a fighting man. To my way of seeing it, he was the spirit of war, whether we liked it or not, and even whether he liked it or not.

Then came the movie, *Sergeant Mills*, which made less of the event itself——the film's promoters were eager to tell the public that in the movie the carnage in the two barracks took exactly the time it was estimated that Mills had taken, four minutes, including a thirty-second walk from the first barracks to the second——than of Mills's life leading up to those two hundred and forty seconds of god-like, almost supernatural death-dealing, and his life in the aftermath, overshadowed by those raging, deafening, almost timeless minutes during which he was Death itself.

When the film came out, Millsy was 91 and in an old people's home in Cromer, where the pub that he'd run for thirty years after the war (he was 42 when the war ended, and only too glad to be demobbed) now suddenly had its name changed from 'The Gilded Otter' to 'The Sergeant Major.' He welcomed my visit, he said, as a change from the reporters who were treating him with a strange mixture of respect——as though he might leap from his wheelchair and liquidate them too——and disgust, as if he were some ancient scorpion found alive in a pharaoh's tomb.

I asked, as I fear the reporters must have done before me, if there was any element of vindication in all the fuss to which he was now being treated, at last.

Millsy shook his head, amused. "At my age, son, I'm entirely focused on the little space," he raised a hand in front of his now famous, trademark spectacles, and created an inch of distance between his thumb and middle finger, "between myself and death. In that space, every day is good. But it has bugger all to do with who I once was. That seems so long ago it could be someone else that kicked those barracks doors down. They did a good job of reconstruction in the film, I'll say that. But I still couldn't remember how it felt. It was someone else, that Sergeant-Major Mills. Anyway, it's no use to me now, all this attention. It's as useless to me as money. Fame's good for two things, Runt. Impressing women, and annoying your friends. Far as I'm concerned, it's too late to impress women, and my friends are all dead. One day you'll know what I mean, if you don't already."

Having just celebrated my 78th birthday, I had an inkling.

6. *France*

ON THE EVE OF THE BATTLE OF SCHULTHEIM young Bernhard Forsmann had a vision, in a dream, of an encounter on the battlefield. A young Danish soldier jumped down into the muddy pit where Bernhard was preparing for battle. They stared at each other, weapons drawn, and in that endless instant, in the dream, Bernhard pictured the other man's life. Newly married to a foreigner, the fiery daughter of an Italian weaver, the boy in front of him had endured the hostility of his own and his bride's family. Bernhard knew that in the next instant either he would be dead at the Danish soldier's hands and, after moments of dreadful pain, lie buried in the muddy trench, perhaps never to be discovered, or the Dane would be dead. The Dane's Italian wife, Bernhard understood in the dream, would swiftly marry another man, an Italian, they would have children, and her first, Danish husband would never be mentioned. At last she herself would forget that she had ever married him. In the dream vision, as the two men faced each other, Bernhard felt words welling up*: I don't want to fight you.* Although he didn't speak the words aloud, he imagined the Danish soldier echoing them. As an immense wave of relief swept over him, he felt himself frame a further sentence. *We can be brothers.* Far from seeming like a hackneyed, sentimental utterance, it seemed to him at that moment immense and urgent; it was as if he had thrown off the entire curse of war and the sacrifice of nameless millions. He saw them in his dream, a horde advancing as some fell to arrows they never saw coming, lives extinguished like a candle.

By this act of sparing a life, the dream told Bernhard, you have endowed mankind with the work this Danish boy will accomplish, later in life, which would otherwise have died with him, unimagined and unachieved. What this discovery was, or this invention, or work of art or poetry, Bernhard woke to find the dream had never told him.

To be exact: *I* woke to find this, and to find that I wasn't Bernhard Forsmann, as I had been in the dream. I wasn't Bernhard anybody (and there was, so far as I know, no 'battle of Schultheim' in human history), I was Runt Rawlinson, I was in France on my third mission, and one of the strangest things about my dream, stranger than the fading intensity of having resolved war itself by a gesture of sheer brotherhood, by offering the enemy my hand——(much good that would do when the Gestapo came to take me away)——was that my dreaming self had invented for me another man's name.

It's true that my dream life expanded luridly when I was on a mission, or perhaps my memory of my dreams increased, and either this or the profusion of dreams in itself was perhaps attributable, I thought, both to the tensions of the day and the difficulty I had in sleeping, as well as the shallowness of my sleep when I did sleep. We were on guard all the time, on a mission, and rarely slept properly until we were off enemy soil.

And perhaps this particular dream, with its 'Bernhard Forsmann' identity (interesting that I seemed to be a German, as if my subconscious were willing my nemesis to offer brotherhood instead of death) had to do with the fact that I was carrying a false name, as always in the field. In this case it was Jean-Louis Garçonnier——a ridiculous name, meaning 'boyish' or conceivably 'boyo', one of

Uncle Reggie's favourite words, or might be thought to refer, as does the word *garçonnière*, to a bachelor apartment or one designated for clandestine use by lovers——a name which had not been mockingly coined by F Section but had belonged to a real family of gentleman farmers in the region. They were primed, I was told, to act as my reception committee when I parachuted onto their land under cover of night, and would vouch for me, if necessary, as a distant cousin, newly arrived.

It was the mission I'd been waiting for, all along. No linking up with partisans or *franc-tireurs* of dubious allegiance, no meetings to promote a new network, no recruiting. There would be no contact at all with undercover colleagues whether English or French. I was going on my own, without even a courier to relay news and bolster my spirits. (Or to fuck, as in many instances unrecorded by SOE historians. Our couriers were mostly women. We were told that this was because women were less conspicuous than males of military age. Condemned men that we were, or felt ourselves to be, we knew better. Our courier-visits were our last meal and, if they were willing, we were grateful.)

This one was a *bolo* mission as we called it, for reasons that escape me. It may have had something to do with the South American *bolo* lariat, weighted with stones, that can be retrieved after wrapping itself around its victim's legs and returns to base intact, as the *bolo* agent hopes to do, like a boomerang after completing its mission. Or it may simply have been the word *solo* combined with any of a dozen uncomplimentary adjectives beginning with 'b'.

After the business in the Tarn, when my radio transmission was traced (or I was betrayed by one of my *réseau*, I never knew which and don't know to this day) and I was arrested and only escaped thanks to my captors' greed and my ample supply of francs, I wasn't sure I'd get another go. Close shaves often crippled people's nerve, and I couldn't yet be sure what, if anything, it had done to mine. Neither could 'F' section be sure, which was probably why they sent me on a bolo, where I couldn't compromise anyone else if I screwed up. I was even given a choice. You can say no, Runt, Uncle Reggie said. "You've done your bit, and if it's of any interest to you there might soon be a red and blue ribbon on your chest or, knowing you, chucked in a foot-locker somewhere." He was telling me I was already up for the Distinguished Service Order, as I'd half suspected, and that there was no need for any further derring-do if it was a medal I was after. Most of us got the DSO if we'd been out to France a time or two and managed not to mess up. But when he said it was a bolo mission I didn't hesitate. 'Anita,' this one was called, and it would also be my codename. Most bolos were in-and-out jobs with a single target, sometimes a sabotage target, sometimes human. I think I'd been hoping all along for a chance to be an assassin (not just in the SOE but all my life, since childhood). I'd never indicated as much, of course, because SOE didn't like to think they were employing sickos or freaks, even though that's just who they were seeking to recruit. And no doubt it really was better to pretend otherwise.

'Anita' was indeed an assassination run, as it turned out, and I was glad of it. No-one to mess things up for me. All on my head, free and clear. I felt as if this, much more than the contact-making work I'd done before, was what I'd joined up for. If you'd asked me I'd've said it was what I was made for.

Can you imagine a person who *wanted* to become an assassin? I'm not sure I can, now. But that was me, in those days. Perhaps it's a runt's dream; or perhaps in my childhood alongside Gérard I had so thoroughly inhaled the glamour of crime and so completely embraced the idea of my own doom that all I could legitimately wish for was to wind these two elements around each other and push them to the limit.

ANITA RAN LIKE clockwork to begin with. The steady old 'tortoise', as we called the Stirling bomber, dropped a ton of supplies over the Bordeaux area (my old *réseau*, so I knew who'd be there down on the ground, gathering up the boxes in the dark of night), leaving me alone in the cavernous fuselage. I was the final delivery, and landed rather peacefully in sloping pasture. The ground was soft, which not only made for a better landing but made spadework easier. Once I'd buried my chute suit and the chute itself I sat down and waited, trusting my reception committee to have been scanning the skies and spotted me. Soon enough it showed up, in the form of an old man who called to me from the treeline, *"Venez, Monsieur! Venez!"* For the rest of my stay at Garçonnier Towers, a ramshackle place whose real name was Labaronnerie, the old boy continued to address me with a combination of sign language and primitive French spoken loudly and slowly, no matter how fluently I spoke to him, even using his own patois. Albert was his name, mine was Monsieur, and from the beginning I dreaded what would happen if a militiaman showed up to question him about me. Albert was not made, it seemed to me, for espionage. But somehow he had been induced by the local *réseau* to enter into this adventure, and I had to bless him for it.

Albert always dressed like a gardener anticipating muddy work, and when he brought me back to Labaronnerie that first night I expected him to leave me in the stone-flagged hall, where the Garçonnier clan would be awaiting me. Instead he trudged on steadily round to the kitchen entrance and there offered me tea, bread and butter that he churned in secret (butter! I hadn't seen butter for three years) and a great deal of Albert sign language. Finally, after much questioning and much shaking of Albert's shaggy white head, I grasped that there was no Garçonnier clan. He was it. Albert was the patriarch and everyone else was either dead, which included his wife and two sons, or they were elsewhere, which comprised two more sons, who I trusted were working for the Resistance rather than the Germans. Just you? I asked. No-one else living here? Only you? Albert nodded. Who runs the farm? I asked. My concern was less for the amount of work this might be causing him than for a workforce from whom I might have to conceal my presence. But Albert just stared back at me. What do you take me for? his gaze seemed to say. You think I can't run my own farm?

He did, rising at four to prepare the cows' feed, milking them by hand and then dispatching them unaided into the fields, before taking to his tractor to work the arable land. I was happy to picture Albert busy and unmindful of his visitor, while I made my way into town to hunt down ODG, as I had come to call him, in my mind. My target, Olivier du Greffand.

I HAD LOGGED everything we knew about ODG, which wasn't all that much. (Besides which our dossiers were notorious for containing arrant nonsense, either misplaced or imported from sources talking through their backside.) What was beyond dispute was that he was a Communist and a *maquisard*, one of those Resistance men who, when De Gaulle pronounced them all *Forces Françaises de L'Intérieur,* even before the Normandy Landing and before there *was* a French *intérieur* again, rejected the title, wanting nothing to do with that ridiculous imperial poseur and self-appointed saviour, as they saw him. In civil life du Greffand was a doctor, a respected member of the community, and had been liaising with 'F' section since '41. Indeed he was one of the founding members of the troubled Montfort *réseau*. With the return to Britain of Teapot Armfield, after his famous trash-bin escape from Buchenwald, we discovered just why it was that the Montfort *réseau* had been so troubled, losing numerous members to arrest, torture and death. One of these was Marie Marquand, a Polish girl who had achieved the status of an icon at SOE. Marie had certainly been an icon for me. I had adored her from afar——her sexual affiliation had always been a matter for speculation among us, and though some said she had none, I suspected she had placed it temporarily in the freezer, like everything else in her life except for her SOE functions. She was waiting, we told ourselves, to conclude her vendetta against the Nazis. If it ever could be concluded; the Gestapo had killed Marie's father and younger sister, and I wondered whether anything, Hitler's downfall or even the extermination of the entire German race would serve to dowse her flame. I think it was precisely her lack of romantic interest in any of us, combined with her skills, her magnetism and attractiveness, that made her our idol and our saint. She worked harder than anyone. She was the best shot, famously so, in the SOE, and at exactly five foot tall could beat any of us over an obstacle course.

And *monsieur* ODG, it turned out, had betrayed her to the Germans. I couldn't wait to kill him.

Of course, if we'd gone round trying to pick off every traitor or suspected traitor on enemy soil we'd have had no-one left to fight the enemy, and frankly if it hadn't been

Marie Marquand he'd betrayed I doubt if we'd have bothered setting up a hit in this way. I learned later that the 'Anita' mission was approved in council by just one vote, and that only a phone call from Churchill swayed some determined opposition at the highest levels of SOE. Whether this was because they disapproved of the precedent 'Anita' was setting, one of expending human resources on execution, or weren't entirely convinced by Armfield's information, I've never discovered. Teapot's account of Marie's betrayal came at second hand, since he hadn't met Marie after her arrest but only heard the story of it from a courier who was arrested with her.

She was born Marie Maciejski in Poznan, not 'Marquand,' which was an F Section invention. And now we'd learned that she was dead, shot at Niederland transit camp with three of our couriers, all of them girls. I was proud of F Section for refusing to let her betrayal simply disappear into the roll call of similar tragedies. And this ODG, this bastard du Greffand, according to the report, had not only betrayed her but presided over the transmissions that Marie had been forced to make (or that ODG had made for her, as seemed to us far more likely) after three days of incarceration and torture in the basement of du Greffand's house.

That basement already haunted me. I didn't want to see it, and yet I did, and if possible I wanted to kill du Greffand there, after a few reprisals of my own devising.

It was an unlikely scenario, of course. Getting into du Greffand's house was a possibility, but it might entail risks not incurred by placing my Welrod against his head in a deserted street. I loathed the Welrod, one of our boffin-inspired gadgets. Its name derived from its Welwyn Garden City origins, Boffin City as it was for us, but we all referred to the gun as the illrod after we'd seen it fail, once, on the firing range. Once was enough. It was a single-shot pistol that could be packed flat and even when assembled made no bulge in the pocket. If you held it against the victim's head when you pulled the trigger it made virtually no sound. This was excellent, except that a single-shot pistol can't afford to jam, even once, and as for a silencer that only worked when the gun was held against a victim's head, only a Welwyn Garden City boffin could dream up a victim unfailingly willing to comply. *Hold still please, this won't hurt a bit.*

Never mind the illrod. I had my trusty cheesewire. There were a lot of ways to kill a man. All you really needed was the desire. I had the L-pill, too, L for lethal (I dare say D-pill for death was thought too grim), which I couldn't help thinking of as the Love pill. I'd certainly love to pop it down ODG's throat.

"We could have asked the locals to dispatch *monsieur* traitor," Uncle Reggie had told me laconically, "but we knew how much you'd enjoy it, so we left him to you." The truth was, of course, that we couldn't trust any of the locals to do it or even to believe our story about du Greffand. In all likelihood the very person we'd try to contact to get the job done would be an ally of du Greffand's, who would promptly warn him that we had his number. The whole of the Montford *réseau* might be compromised, for all we knew, and certainly they had to be treated as if this was so, in a matter of this kind. *Make an example of him,* the P.M. had apparently said of the 'Anita' mission's target, in his decisive phone call. We were to take the manifest trouble to send someone in to kill him, as a warning to all other potential traitors. Marie was understood to have been one of Churchill's favourites. Now I was the man chosen to avenge Marie, and Churchill. It was heady stuff. I was the SOE and Britain's champion, a David sent out to tackle the Goliath of the traitorous French Philistines.

THE TOWN LIES roughly six kilometres away from Labaronnerie by road, less than this if (as I was to discover) you take a route through the empty Garçonnier fields. Walking into town that first day, I could taste revenge, and I kept Marie's image in my mind. I pictured her as the SS guards pushed her forwards, wearing some shapeless cotton shift, through a doorway and into a courtyard where the telltale bullet holes in the brick wall make it all too clear what has happened here before and is about to happen to them. Marie, I knew, would be trying to keep the other girls' strength up. Would their hands be free, so that at least she could hold the hand of the girl on either side? In the final instants she would be thinking of her father and her sister. Perhaps it wouldn't be happening in a courtyard but in a field outside the camp, the four girls each standing over their grave awaiting the customary SS shot in the back of the head. Now, in my mind, all four are holding hands. Now the shots, and now they fall, lifeless, these brave, fine, honourable souls.

ODG, here I come.

Town streets are the right place to be, the right place to hunt, where the gloom rules that descended on the look of things, soon after the war began, as if some dark force more insidious than Nazism had already penetrated and conquered us all.

It's market day, as I knew before I landed here, and now, just as I hoped, I find myself drifting towards the market square along with the rest of the human flotsam, who look as depressed as if they'd been under Nazi rule for 50 years instead of less than three. (We had a professor come and lecture us at Beaulieu on The Psychology of

Defeat. He was a Pole, this professor. If Marie Maciejski hadn't been present that day, in between missions, I think I might have been tempted to point out that as a Pole he probably had a head start on the rest of us when it came to understanding defeat.) Looking up, I see a small tree of some sort poking its sad snout out of a crevice at the very top of a house, just under the roof; if you leaned out of the mansard window above it, the window jutting from the eaves, you could lean down and wrestle it out or cut it off. Everything else in the little street is drably orderly. It's hard to remember how riotous the French are, indoors, with a little drink in them, standing on tables and pouring wine on each other's heads and cheering each other on to send more down their gullet, *et glou et glou et glou!* Their exteriors, though, their streets, are perfect for fascism, sombre and unmemorable. As bad as Britain, really. Why are we fighting Fascism when we've already given in to it, heads bowed in ugly uniformity? The shock of a girl's pale body, more the colour and the fact of it, before you even touch its nakedness——the shock preserved in memory no less than the shock in reality, at the time——tells us how grim and grey we've become. The girl spread out against the sheets, lying back, languid. My mind always goes there just before a drop or when the action's about to begin, and if I have time I dare say it'll go there when I'm dying.

I don't need to follow the human flotsam, but doing so helps me imagine that I'm part of the town, that I belong here. I already know where the market square is because I've studied a map of the town closely enough to be able to walk it blindfold. The first day is always the same. You feel like a well-equipped alien from another planet who can't yet quite believe, despite the evidence of his reflection in shop windows, that he really looks like someone from planet Earth. I know without checking that

I'm dressed appropriately, because one of Netta's most invaluable contributions to our work in the field is the ever-elaborated and updated catalogue she makes of current fashions (yes, even in wartime) and customs. This library of ephemera ranges from the stupidly obvious——one of our agents was arrested after he ordered a *café noir* in a metropolitan area that hadn't seen milk in eighteen months——to the arcane, such as the latest slang, newspaper tidbits or the most popular lines from the new Becker or Clouzot film. I know I'm in good shape (in terms of conformity) in my baggy blue trousers and old tweed jacket, but to make sure of this I catch the eye of a few farmers as I enter the crowded market, and see that for an instant they think they know me. Then, realizing they don't, they look away without a further thought. The eyes of an elderly, overweight veterinarian, trimming the hooves of a dairy goat while its owner clings to the animal's head with all her might, rests on mine a little longer, but only out of idle curiosity. I fit in almost too well, which makes people try and remember who I am. In a small town, however, the only alternative to this is to look out of place.

The sense of being onstage, the focus of all eyes, even though you know quite well you're not, is palpable. Even without the presence of specific danger, everything is running a little slower already, the downy little chicken feathers held aloft in the breeze as farmers unpack their crated fowl hang there even more like a frozen frame. I'm back. My panoramic sense of detail is back. I'm queasy and tense and aglow with this peripheral awareness that only fear, at a visceral, animal level, can summon, yet as relaxed (I remind myself) as any martial artist practitioner. I'm on the spot, longing for it to be over and wanting it never to end.

The star is back——I suppose that's what I really mean and what I wanted to hear from Millsy, V.C., too. *I wondered if there was anything in the world I couldn't do, that day.* All of your life you're an extra, aside from moments like these. The training I'd loved to distraction, but with my first mission an alternation re-entered my life, a species of sub-clinical manic cycle I hadn't known since my schooldays as a juvenile thief. The first mission triggered it again. The mission itself was a shambles ("bit of a fiasco," Reggie had said in an indulgent tone, acknowledging that it hadn't all been my fault), but I was alive as I hadn't been since slipping down a midnight corridor, 3 ack emma was my prowl hour, to penetrate the bedrooms of a snoring world. Moments of living came at me in their foregrounded form, vivid glimpses as still and clear as an epileptic vision. (I've driven though the postwar Landes, revisiting old mission scenes and hoping, unavoidably, for a frisson. None comes, in that dull landscape, which is hardly to blame for having gone back to sleep.) The ivy, I can see it still, on the ridge of a grey stucco'd wall of a featureless suburban house, glittered at me one morning like a nest of open, dark green mouths.

Life between missions, after that first mission, now seemed as sickly as classroom hours had been at school, between midnight excursions. Suddenly I was back in the land of alternation, up-time and down-time. I was as grateful for 'Anita' as an addict for a shot of his favourite poison. After a mission even the sense of touch seemed to atrophy. Whereas, in the field, every sight, even a filament of dust falling in sunlight in a dusty hotel room, seemed like the last glimpse of the world, alive with meaning, intended for you to memorize and parse for ever. It was a drug, and horrible in its way, like a dream demanding attention and retention even as it faded from the senses.

Crowds can be deceptively relaxing. Debouching from a sad side street whose gutters already bear witness to market day, the square itself is an astonishing expanse of light and safety, the safety of a multitude. There's a tremendous bustle in the square, with chickens squawking and struggling and threatening to take off and circle overhead in their crates of wooden slats and wire mesh, there are geese barely under control and more crates full of rabbits, there are cows the size of small cars, and several bulls larger still, and not a sign of a German anywhere. The Polish professor who came to lecture us at Beaulieu had calculated that aside from troops and the SS and Gestapo cadres, the Nazis ran France with less than a hundred people. The rest of it was done by the French themselves, with the added and intermittently visible threat of uniformed Nazi force. Less than a hundred bureaucrats, he said, to our astonished and unbelieving silence. That's all it took, once the good old Psychology of Defeat kicked in. In any case, if it's a choice between the Krauts and the Brits, for a Frenchman, most of them will choose the Krauts. It's in their blood (or in their history at any rate). And some of them, "the highbrow sort," we were told, admire German culture so intensely that they welcomed the war from the beginning, in the hope that France would indeed become a German satellite. This doesn't sound very French, it's true, but I knew first-hand that it wasn't only the "highbrow sort" who admired the Germans. Gérard was mad for them, and owned a German helmet from the first war, the kind with a spike in the crown of it. On occasion he wore it to battle——street fighting, I mean——and charged the enemy head down.

What on earth were we fighting and dying for on French soil, if the French preferred the Germans anyway? This was the thought in every head, I think, when the professor unveiled his statistics. But they *didn't* prefer the Krauts, surely. Not all of them. We had to believe they didn't. They were just cowed and shamed by the swiftness of their defeat. It would be enough to make any nation doubt itself.

Yet they seemed full of beans that Saturday in the market square. Small French children dashed around, heedless of flying hooves and beaks. Townies examined farmers' goods with a canny eye, and bargained ferociously. There was plenty of food on show. Where was the war? You couldn't see it.

At the centre of the square a small temporary enclosure had been set up, where beasts being auctioned could be displayed between movable wooden walls. This is where, that day, disaster nearly occurred, and I'm quite sure it wasn't the first time, the hubbub and the chaos of that Saturday market being what it was. A child, no more than two years old, three at the most, ran into the enclosure, probably not knowing where he was going amid the forest of legs, just as a bull was being ushered out by its new owner and a second bull being dragged in.

Half a dozen hands hauled the heavy wooden gate shut, and then there was a moment of absolute horror, like an intake of breath, before everyone began to shriek at once, seeing that the sawdust-strewn enclosure was now entirely occupied by a small child and a bull weighing at least a ton. The child looked round in bewilderment, seemingly able to see everything except the bull, as if some dispensation of the spirit simply prevented him from registering the company of a creature that, to the child, must have been the size of locomotive. The bull was also alerted by the screams, and raised its head as if wondering what was expected of it. For a moment it pawed the ground, as if absent-mindedly. Then it lowered its head, and saw the child.

What happened next took as long as any moment of danger I'd managed to defuse during a mission, by my old expedient——yet it wasn't an expedient, that's the thing, it happened to me unbidden——of slowing my pulse and living in the gaps between seconds. When this happens I'm always reminded of a short story I read as a young man, because in it the hero is able to stop time entirely, for everyone and everything but himself. He's on a bus at one point, I remember, and is struck by how ugly we are in life, as in a photograph for which we haven't prepared a face, when he looks round the other passengers and sees them all frozen in place (he himself is able to move around freely), including one chap who is caught in the act of winking lewdly at a young woman, and on whose face the wink is stuck in seeming perpetuity. In the same way, I feel a kind of monitory throb in my heart, like a kind of electrical switch, saying, *now*. Everything around me slows down, by no means to the same degree as it does for the man in the short story, but still appreciably. I'm acting in my own time and no-one else's.

At this moment in the market square, I see the gateway push inwards and a small fat man propel himself into the enclosure. I recognize him as the elderly veterinarian who was trimming the goat hooves. Before he can speak, before he can act, even, the bull leaves off pawing the ground and launches itself at the child. In an act of unhesitating bravery, the small, plump old man leaps forward, covers ten feet of ground virtually in the bull's hot, snorting breath and seizes the child, rolling in the sawdust with him as the enormous creature thunders past and slowly wheels for a second charge.

The screaming around us has reached a level which must have been audible to the limits of the town and beyond, perhaps even to old Albert's ears, if he hadn't been on his tractor. A man beside me bellows at the vet as he lies on the ground with the child, trying to get up, and now the old man sees him. Rising, covered in sawdust, he makes towards us with the wriggling and inaudibly screaming child in his arms. But he is slower this time, the little old vet, slower to cover the ground inside the terrible bear-pit of this miniature arena, where the gateway has long since been opened to incite the bull to make his exit——futile endeavour, since the bull has identified his quarry and will not be denied.

As the old man comes towards us holding the child aloft, the bull makes his charge. Now the vet reaches us and the child is seized by its father and hauled, yelling, over the barrier, as the bull gathers speed, reaching the middle of the little ring. As small as I am, I was born, I think, with unusual upper body strength. I discovered this in Montmartre street fights, and I cultivated it in gyms all through my teenage years and into my twenties. Even 'J' was unwilling to arm-wrestle me, or allow himself to get into a position on the mat where he couldn't outmanoeuvre me with leg strength.

I pitch myself onto the barrier in front of me, with its ridge now bending me in half, ready to take lifting-strain in my gut, ready to lean down and seize the old boy, who to judge by his eyes has prepared himself for death, or at least for the broken back and the crippled existence that will ensue when the bull crushes him against the barrier from behind, as in less than a second he will. Catching the vet under his arms and hoisting him as high as I can in one do-or-die lift, I feel the bull's head hit the barrier with all his might, flinging the entire assemblage——myself, the old man, and the section of wooden siding——backwards into the crowd.

Pandemonium ensues, and all is legs and arms and clothes and continued screaming, and while we are picking ourselves out of the debris, a number of ropes lassoo the frustrated bull (one good bolo could have done the trick and joined two of his legs together!). By what appears to everyone to have been a miracle inspired by the vet's extraordinary courage, no-one is hurt, no-one is scarred. A drama for dinnertime consumption, a tale to be told and re-told for generations, has been etched into town lore, with no harm done.

"*Mes félicitations, monsieur*," I congratulate the vet.

"*Ah*," he says, still panting, "*C'est moi, monsieur*," returning the congratulations, adding that I undoubtedly saved his life.

When we reach the stage of mutual introductions I have my first opportunity to test drive my Garçonnier identity. The little old roly poly fellow knows Albert, as I expected, and is more than ready to believe, it seems, that so evidently obliging a distant cousin as myself has arrived to help old Garçonnier run the farm, now that none of Albert's sons are available.

"Will you come to supper tomorrow?" the old boy asks. "Please. I beg you. My wife will hardly forgive me, when she hears the story of our adventure today, unless I invite you."

"By all means."

"Excellent. My name is du Greffand," he adds, and whether I'm able to keep all reaction out of my face I have no idea, but I rather doubt it. "Olivier du Greffand, at your service."

7. *Dimanche en ville*

IT WAS SPLENDID. I COULD NEVER have devised a better way to get into the man's house. Of course, I'm anxious to keep my mind trained on this aspect of the day's discoveries, rather than on the apparent misinformation in ODG's SOE dossier (not just a 'doctor,' thank you very much, colleagues, but specifically a *vet*, you idiots, a *veterinarian*), never mind reflecting that on arrival at my destination, with the unambiguous instruction to track down and kill a traitor, the very first thing I do on entering the town where he lives is to save his life. Dear God, the bull might have done my job for me, if only I'd let it.

If only I'd known.

But then, of course, I wouldn't get the pleasure myself.

Nor do I want to think about the man's bravery. Can one be an odious traitor and torturer, and yet a brave man who risks his life for a child? Certainly. But too bad. *Tant pis.* For his crimes he must die, and die cruelly if I have any choice.

I spent Sunday doing my own private drill. There were recommended procedures but I'm sure that regardless of what we told our trainers everyone had his own way of keeping mind and body occupied and agile during tedious hours of waiting. I liked to alternate press-ups with map work and code work, as well as checking all equipment, including the radio, and dissassembling and reassembling the wretched Welrod, using my chronometer to time myself.

One thing I had to work hard on in the code work part of my drill, perhaps harder than some other agents who had a knack for it, was memorizing the poem or section of a poem (a new one, of course, each time) which had been chosen to serve as our code book for a particular mission, and which, by assigning to each letter of the alphabet its number from 1 to 26, would identify a letter in the poem corresponding to each letter of our message, and yield an encoded version. Obviously we couldn't keep a written-out version of the poem, since if it was found it would enable the finder to broadcast using the code, so even those of us who were rotten at poetry had to memorize it. This meant using fairly easy or familiar poems, because if an agent was unable to remember a part of it, or misremembered so much as a word, it could garble the whole message. Worse still, if someone in the field went completely blank on their poem, they might be unable to arrange to be picked up at the end of their mission, and wind up sending uncoded signals, in desperation, which home base could hardly answer in uncoded form, to arrange a rendez-vous, since this would jeopardize the pilot's life as well as the agent's. There were tales of agents never heard from again, of whom it was suspected that far from having been the victim of foul play, disposed of without trace, they'd panicked when they lost track of their code work, and fled to Spain. At least one was later said to have surfaced after the war, with a new identity. Some just went doolally in the middle of a mission and broadcast the name of a new poem, one they could remember and would now use——absurdly, having announced to the listening Germans what the code would be——to encode their message. People did all kinds of daft things in the field. Even when they didn't virtually deliver the code in person to Nazi HQ, as in the case of transmitting an unencoded message announcing a new code poem, the Germans were onto us. They quickly found out we were using poems, and came to realize that the British field agent's repertoire of the poetry he was unlikely to forget could be fitted into a very slim volume indeed. Much as we ourselves would have done (only using widely familiar German verse) if Hitler's codes had been drawn from poetry his undercover agents could memorize, the Abwehr scoured Palgrave's Treasury and other sources of childhood rote learning, hoping to reduce the permutations they had to apply to our messages.

'Kubla Khan' and 'Jabberwocky,' both well supplied with the letters we most needed, were also just the kind of stuff the Germans were now expecting. We retaliated by creating our own 'poems' out of famous lines in a new order, or using simple doggerel cadences, easy to remember but not to be found in any book. This more or less eliminated German chances of breaking our codes, but it increased our own chances of forgetting the 'poem.' In the end we got a new code chappie in to completely redesign our approach, thank God. But 'Anita' was one of the last missions under the old dispensation, and I had begged to be given a real poem, even if it was a relatively obscure one, rather than one of Reggie's home-made 'poems,' which tended to run something like, *Tra la la, tra la lee, the pig jumped over the moon, the cook and her lover ran off to sea, and the rat ran away with the spoon.* Anyone who could remember this kind of all-but-familiar gibberish fully deserved the DSO, in my view.

Reggie knew my opinion of his 'poems'and, out of pure spite, when I demanded something different, he set me a Shakespeare sonnet instead, which I must admit I can remember to this day. *When to the sessions of sweet silent thought*, it begins, *I summon up remembrance of things past, I sigh the lack of many a thing I sought, and with old woes new wail my dear time's waste.*

My God, I had to work on this, though. I never did sort out whether the *past/waste* rhyme was just the Bard's idea of an up-yours to sonneteering or whether the Elizabethans pronounced *past* 'paste' or *waste* 'wast'. I still don't know. My English master at Merchant Taylors told us, I think, that Shakespeare spoke in a mixture of Staffordshire and West Country with some other accent, I forget what, thrown in. Try as I might with these flavours added, I still couldn't make *past* and *waste* rhyme. I even began to imagine that Uncle Reggie had picked this poem for me precisely because of an unhelpful rhyme early on. But I turned this thought around. Didn't it make the poem extra memorable, because of the bad rhyme? I'd better think that way, I told myself, or I'd be lost.

The whole pressure of a bolo mission, for me at least, was precisely that there was no-one around to prompt me if I forgot the damn poem. It was more of a worry to me——far more——than the question of how I was going to kill my target and accomplish my mission. For most people, I dare say, a murder would be a more worrisome prospect than memorizing a sonnet. For me it was the other way around. Any fool could cut a man's throat, but remembering fourteen lines of Shakespeare pushed me to the limit. I was a little French boy till I was 13, I wanted to cry out! I was Alain, I came to all this stuff, in fact to the English language itself, late! I must have repeated that damn sonnet (it's number 30 if you feel like looking it up and suffering all the way through it with me) at least once every fifteen minutes during the first few days of 'Anita,' when I was on my own.

I can see myself stalking across the Garçonnier acres in the fading light, reciting the sonnet over and over, on the way in to have dinner with du Greffand and his wife, and as I do so I'm whipping off the heads of frothing cow parsley with a switch, decimating them like so many treacherous double agents, torturers posing as heroic veterinarians. I'm not expecting to do anything violent to ODG that evening; plenty of time. And I am marginally concerned, since I gave him my Garçonnier identity and discussed old Albert with him before discovering that he was du Greffand, that he might have identified me to others as the chap who rescued him. This would leave a trail to Albert when I eventually disappeared.

Flax, or something like flax, is spuming into the low-lying, almost horizontal evening sunlight as I beat the tall weeds in the rough Garçonnier pasture. So light that it floats, shimmering in the air like a host of insects disturbed at bedtime, the cottony substance is all around me.

With every step I can feel a raw cut on my calf stinging in an almost pleasing, provocative way——as I fell back into the crowd with du Greffand and the wooden siding on top of me, something sharp, the corner of a little crate perhaps that somebody was carrying, bit into the back of my leg——and I pause and bend down to scratch at it through my baggy trousers, while still mumbling my Shakespeare. The airborne flax is so vivid! At the same time as you revel in the beauty of it, enhanced by danger so near, perhaps, because you never know when you might be walking into a trap, your mind swims at the contrast. It's both sublime and utterly absurd to be walking this glorious indifferent pasture busy with its own affairs, with flying creatures making their last sorties, with flowers settling down to sleep, while each step takes you nearer to what might be ambush, death, the end of it all. Why such alarums? Why couldn't we all just sit down together in this sweet sloping pasture——(*'We can be brothers!'*)——and praise eternity?

Perhaps I'm really more anxious about my mission than I'm inclined to realize; more nervous, now that I'm contemplating the assassination of a newly-acclaimed local hero. More confused than I want to acknowledge, given that I saved his life without a second's hesitation. Perhaps I'm reciting Shakespeare not as my code-source lifeline home but as if it were a spell, standing between me and the reality of 'Anita'.

When to the sessions of sweet silent thought....

THE SAD-SNOUT TREE, poking its way out under the gutter, is waiting for me in the twilight. For a moment, counting house numbers along the street, I think it is that very house, the one with the secret tree-lodger, that is du Greffand's.. But my number arrives first, three doors away. It's a house of a colour beyond the wit of even a paint company to designate, a faintly yellowish mixture of cream, grey and olive drab, with a front door of faintly pebbled glass bearing what seems like a wrought iron door set into the glass, or between two heavy, equally tall glass panes. The kind of door you might expect to see fronting a French doctor's consulting rooms. And indeed there are two names with medical titles on plaques set into the wall, beneath du Greffand's. I'm pleased to discover that he seems to be a proper medical doctor, as per my information, but not sure what to make of the other names. Does he rent a floor of his house to them, perhaps?

An intercom system and an automatic, buzzer-accompanied release permits me to open the front door and, when I go in, to hear du Greffand's cheerful voice echoing down the stairwell tells me to come up to the third floor, where his apartment is.

Where then, I wonder as I climb the broad stairs, equipped with more fine wrought iron for its balustrade, and winding in a spiral around an *ascenseur* (which I don't take, having been leery of lifts all my life), is the basement where Marie was held and abused? Is there a basement in the building at all? If there is, would ODG have unlimited access to it, with no chance that anyone would blunder in and interrupt him? Perhaps this was another inaccuracy. Perhaps the basement was somewhere quite else. Or it was all an error and there wasn't a basement involved at all.

I reach the *troisième*, am ushered in, introductions and drinks follow, and then we sit down to a frugal but rather exquisite meal, served not by Mme du Greffand but by a servant who also cooks. We eat on a fine lace-trimmed tablecloth the colour of lard, and make polite conversation about the availability of various foodstuffs. I draw on my familiarity with the Tarn-et-Garonne region, where I supposedly live when not helping out my *Oncle* Albert (my cousin, supposedly, but an honorary uncle in view of his age). I compare the hardships of my own region. We discuss Albert, and I discover that it is Madame du Greffand who is locally born and bred and has known the Garçonnier family (to whom I bear an evident resemblance, she insists) all her life. Olivier du Greffand is a blow-in from the Corrèze, where he was raised on a farm. Hence, I am given to understand, his nostalgia and fondness for treating animals, and his willingness to act as stand-in vet on market days. He is by trade a general practitioner, already overworked.

We are so polite and discreet, unwilling to probe, that it's hard to gauge anything about du Greffand. Politics doesn't come up at all. The Germans are not mentioned,

There is no war. (Overhearing our dinner table, you might really think there wasn't.) I know I have to break into this mannerliness. Meanwhile I wonder whether the man is, perhaps, one of those who succeeds in hiding his entire undercover life from his wife? It's possible. Of course she could be privy to the whole of it and in the presence of a stranger there might be no hint given at all.

We return, inevitably, to the gladiatorial moments in the little ring on Saturday, and as Mme du Greffand begins a long, genealogically dense exposition of why it had to be that particular toddler, of all the toddlers from all the various families in the town, who would have run into the auction ring and got himself trapped with the bull, I put on a smile, retreat into my head, and try to sum up what I've gleaned about *Monsieur* Target so far.

The news is mixed, some of it gratifying and some of it troubling. On the gratifying side, there's at least one piece of information confirming du Greffand as *the* du Greffand. It's not a common name, and as unlikely as it is that another Olivier du Greffand lives in the town, it would be far from impossible that this Olivier might have a son called Olivier who also practices medicine, and it would be just like SOE to assassinate the wrong one. But this Dr. du Greffand has no offspring, it turns out. A little probing about the du Greffand name——making Olivier spell it out for me——has allowed me to ask if the surname is widespread here, and I've discovered that to his knowledge there isn't another du Greffand for a hundred miles in any direction. And since the Olivier du Greffand sitting before me, my Olivier du Greffand, is indeed a medical doctor, SOE has scored at least one direct hit.

As for the bad news, I'm not sure I can estimate how troubling it is until I get home and turn it over in my mind. There's the absence of a du Greffand house with a basement, as promised, the basement being where ODG purportedly kept Marie Marquand prisoner and subject to torture, before obtaining from her the code poem she was using to encode her messages and, more importantly the secret word with which each field operative was equipped, to slip into their message as a guarantee that they were not broadcasting under coercion.

I should mention that no-one thought any the worse of Marie for having surrendered this information, under torture. Even the most rigorous training can't prepare you for having your head held under water repeatedly, to the point of losing consciousness, by someone who really doesn't much care whether he kills you or not. We were in no hurry to pass judgement on anyone's capacity to hold out. And we knew that most captured agents took to their grave the secret of what they did or did not reveal, since it was in the Germans' interest always to maintain that they had broken under torture whether this was true or not. So in all likelihood no-one would ever find out even if you allowed them to kill you before you gave in.

But in Marie's case something more unpleasant was occurring, typical, alas, of SOE's increasing incompetence as it grew larger and more frantic in its activities, and as the Normandy landings approached and it became of paramount urgency to disrupt German occupying forces in any way we could. We took our eye off communications, to be honest. So that someone simply wasn't paying attention when Marie Marquand, after being captured and presumably having been tortured into revealing the code poem, was forced to broadcast a message to us in code but pointedly failed to include the secret 'security' or 'all clear' word, which in her case happened to have been the word *iron*.

We never discovered the truth of what happened next, until after the war, when some of the horrible mistakes and the sickeningly ruthless, deliberate sacrifices of life gradually emerged out of the shadow of the necessary lies of wartime. Previously, in '43, we were fed an explanation whereby Marie was simply broken and temporarily 'turned' and gave the Germans all the info they needed. The reality had been quite different. Instead of realizing that Marie was being used by the Germans, as the absence of the 'all clear' word indicated, the idiot of a London operator who received Marie's message wrote back as if to a negligent pupil, saying, *add iron to all messages*. If he'd been a smart, wary person, you might think du Greffand, receiving this, would have assumed it was a trap, and that perhaps there was in fact an 'all clear' word other than *iron*, and that by adopting and enclosing *iron* in the messages he sent in Marie's name he would confirm that he wasn't Marie. It seems, though, that Marie's captor was even smarter than that. He actually guessed that this answer was naïve and incompetent on London's part, rather than a cunning trap. In doing this he was putting into practice one of my own maxims, one that in my instructor guise I passed on to my trainees. Allow for the possibility that your enemy is smarter than you are, I used to say, but don't bank on it. He's probably as stupid as you are.

The fact that there is apparently no basement attached to the du Greffand abode, as described in my dossier, is a minuscule glitch compared to the *add iron* communication and to the normal human cock-ups that attended all missions. Marie might have been held and tortured here in the apartment, or in another house somewhere else, with or without a basement, and only remotely connected to du Greffand other than by his use of it for interrogations. Forget the house-with-a-basement business, I tell myself.

Not so easy to dismiss is the matter of ODG's age. This is the first time I've had a chance to take a calm look at du Greffand. I'd paid little attention to him the day before in the market square, other than sizing him up in a general way as a small, portly old man with a battered medical bag, until he told me his name. And then I was so astonished that I spent more time keeping my own face straight than studying his. Now, looking at him under the dim, slightly yellowish interior light of his apartment—— which is actually quite a flattering light, and smooths out wrinkles that are more noticeable by daylight——I'm struck by something more disturbing than the absence of a house and basement as specified in my ODG dossier. The dossier describes him as a man 'in his early fifties.' He was certainly vigorous enough in the sawdust ring while saving the child's life, but now, sitting before me, he's either aged prematurely or he's the image of a man in his mid to late sixties.

Still, it would not be unthinkable for someone referred to as 'age 27' in an OSE dossier to turn out to be 72. So it's foolish, I reminded myself, to place too much weight on any single detail in the dossier. The overwhelming fact was that a Dr Olivier du Greffand had betrayed and tortured Marie, and that here in front of me is the one and only Dr Olivier du Greffand in the region.

So what if as the evening wore on I'm obliged to note that other, minor aspects of the reported du Greffand also lack confirmation? (Where did they get the dossier from anyway? The name of the man who betrayed Marie presumably came from one source, an SOE source who shared the information with another captured SOE operative who managed to escape, while the details came perhaps from *maquisard* sources, and didn't I know myself how unreliable the French were?) It was mentioned in

ODG's dossier that the man had been a champion racing motorcyclist in his youth and even now traveled by motorbike when visiting his patients in outlying, rural regions. While discussing the geographical extent of du Greffand's doctoring responsibilities, I ask whether as a doctor he's able to obtain petrol coupons in order to ensure his mobility, and he tells me he never learned to drive a car, and so has no use for petrol. He uses a bicycle. A pedal-bicycle, occasionally, to go fishing or to visit a patient. A motorbicycle would be faster, I venture, but Hélène du Greffand gives a low chuckle and observes that it would not be faster, if Olivier was riding it. He's not very *sportif*, not the sporting type, she adds. And has enough difficulty staying upright on a pedal bicycle. Hearing this, I resign myself to the irrelevance of my so carefully studied dossier.

Hélène herself is a surprise. There was no mention of a wife in the dossier, but neither need there have been. It's in herself that she's a surprise. I'm not sure why, perhaps ODG's age and self-effacing manner, and his lack of any striking outward charms, but when he'd said. "My wife would never forgive me," as we were standing there on Saturday in the turmoil of market square, dusting down our clothes, I had immediately seen in my mind a little French country mouse who matched him, small and round and a little crabbed. Instead, Mme du Greffand is taller, younger and altogether more voluptuous than I could possible have expected, even if I'd given ODG the benefit of good fortune in the choice of a mate.

Don't misunderstand me. She's younger than I expected but she's not, strictly speaking, young. Perhaps in her middle-to-late forties. If I'm right about our respective ages, she's a good 20 years or so older than me, and something like the same amount younger than her husband. In that sense we almost form three generations as we sit there, the three of us, at the dinner table, while Fernande, the du Greffand's elderly maid of all work and occasional cook, serves us supper. But it doesn't feel like three generations at all. To start with, Hélène du Greffand projects a surly sexuality which seems to run an electrical current around the table and draw everyone into her erotic circuit——her erotic *réseau*——and thereby melt the differences in age between myself and her, as it does between her husband and her. Even Fernande seems attached to Hélène by her own electrical cord, and twitches in intuitive response to her employer's slightest glance. We're all wired up, this is how it feels, to Hélène du Greffand.

How to describe Hélène? Her face can hardly be called pretty, I wouldn't say, though it's certainly imposing. The dark eyes are large and expressive, if somewhat deep-set, giving them a bruised look. An unremarkable nose follows, roundish (the kind of nose I tend to like) rather than sharpish, and then the mouth, like a kind of garish dessert. A raspberry fool, perhaps. It's a mouth you could fall into and drown. Its colour is a dark pink, raspberry-hued indeed, and remarkable for the way the corners of the upper lip fold down, at the edges, in a permanent expression of distaste and disappointment. This is accentuated by the fullness of her lower lip. With a lower lip like this, her mouth seems to be saying, to what stupid, wasteful, ungrateful humiliations must I have been submitted, for my mouth to end up looking like a soggy soufflé, like bread that wouldn't rise, like a duvet too large for its bed and spilling dejectedly onto the floor on either side.

Even when she speaks, this species of collapsed pout that her mouth is still retains its *moue* and its downward twist. When she smiles, the lower lip thins gaily but the upper lip still refuses to lift at the edges and rides the smile out dourly, like a lid on a bubbling pot.

Yet this in itself is a kind of sexual invitation, as every aspect of her mouth seems to be, from its *look-at-me* sulk, at rest, to its sly attempts to escape the surly humbug of its frowning shape. In her otherwise fairly plain face, with her dark, frizzed hair pulled back in a bun, her mouth lives a life of its own, that of a spoiled, bitterly disappointed prima donna exiled to the provinces and the bleak theatre of an unremarkable face (this is what her mouth clearly cannot forgive her other features), and this *diva* of a mouth is determined not to let anyone forget it. Hélène's eyes, I should not forget, have a dark, quiet, talent of their own, and sparkle as if backlit when she's excited. But when this happens, her mouth seems completely unaware (or unwilling to notice) that something interesting is happening on another part of the stage, something quite triumphant and spectacular, in fact. Hélène's mouth doesn't care to know, and retains its sour outline (*I'm a hostage*, it says), closed for business precisely when the rest of her face is most alive.

Along with dessert comes a sweet wine, and with it we toast health, courage and, I insist, good fortune. It's hard not to meet the devil du Greffand's eyes and in doing so renew the bond between us. *On a échappé belle.* We were lucky, in the town square. I know that bond, between two people who've shared a narrow escape, only too well, and the tender look on ODG's face, creasing his little rounded, snubby features with the long upper lip that makes him look a little like some snuffling, rooting forest creature, infuriates me. I force myself to picture his pig-visage sneering at Marie's agonized, drowning face as a German thug lifts her head up out of the water, into the light.

We've drunk quite a bit, I realize. Fernande has been allowed to go home, and now du Greffand breaks out the Vieil Armagnac.

"If there's an emergency you can be sure Olivier will be in the middle of it," Hélène observes, as he pours, in a tone of voice I can't quite penetrate. "It doesn't matter if the patient is human or animal, he's drawn to malady the way some people are drawn to drink. In the middle of the night the phone rings and pffft! He's on his way. If one time he said, take some aspirin, dear, and go back to sleep, I think I'd have a *crise* myself."

"She calls it my addiction," Olivier agrees cheerfully.

"Doctors want to heal the world," Hélène continues. "Even though if they could do it they'd be out of a job. I'd be happy if he settled for healing our street."

"That in itself would take a lifetime, my dear,"

Hélène has already turned to me. "And what is your obsession, *monsieur* Garçonnier?"

"I seem to lack one," I said. "I'm still wondering what it is that life intended me for." We sip our Armagnac. "Perhaps this means I'm destined to be a politician," I say, smiling. It's time to test the water.

Du Greffand chuckles.

Silence falls and for a moment I think I will have to push the boat out farther myself, but Hélène, not her husband, turns out to be my ally. "And what kind of politician would you be, *monsieur* Garçonnier?" she enquires a little tipsily, "*De droite ou de gauche?*" Left or right?

"Certainly not a leftist. I grew up among them and I'm not fooled by their homilies."

"Good for you," Hélène says quietly.

"I wouldn't like to risk giving offense so quickly to new friends, by talking politics," I demur, hoping they'll have forgotten that it was I who raised the subject. I add a barely perceptible glance at Olivier. Pig-visage has contributed nothing since his initial chuckle.

"You couldn't offend Olivier if you tried," Hélène says. "He doesn't believe in politics."

I cradle my Vieil Armagnac, and address my host without trying to seize his attention.

"You don't believe one should take a stand?"

"I believe in individuals, one at a time."

"One case at a time, he means," Hélène corrects, drily. "And all cases equal."

"You think I should treat patients differently according to their politics?"

"Be honest now," Hélène says, "Would you have rushed into that ring today to save Hitler from the bull?"

"*Evidémment,*" Olivier mutters. Of course.

"And de Gaulle too?" She asks.

"Not de Gaulle. He's too big for me." We laugh. "And there would have been no need to rescue de Gaulle. The bull would have kneeled to him."

"I believe Hitler has the right idea," I begin, when our amusement settles. "The Christian principle that we should rescue all weaklings is a foolish one. It's contrary to our self-interest as a species. In the long run I dare say it could even harm us. It defies the logic of our own existence, which has fought tooth and nail to get here. It's why we are here, each of us, regardless of our very excellent capacity for pity."

No-one speaks, but I can feel Hélène's eyes on me.

"As a doctor," I press, smiling, "you must feel that's the devil speaking."

Mildly (the pig is shaking his head) he says, "It's a point of view. It has a great deal to be said for it."

Hélène and I are both gazing at him, and I decide not to risk glancing at her to see whether her expression of patient incredulity matches mine. Is he always so polite? I mean to ask her, but du Greffand is speaking again.

"You speak of logic. But human beings are rarely logical, in my experience. Take you, *monsieur* Garçonnier. Even though you don't believe in such behaviour, you too risked yourself to save a weakling yesterday."

"I did nothing of the kind, *monsieur le docteur*. You're no weakling."

"Did Hitler say that?" Hélène du Greffand asks, without warning.

I've lost the thread, armagnac-soaked, and have to ask her to explain. Did Hitler say what?

"What you said about the dangers of pity. About not rescuing weaklings."

"Certainly," I said, improvisingly as freely as before. "In Bad Gastein, only a few months ago. And he wrote something similar in *Mein Kampf.*"

"You'll have to forgive me," du Greffand broke in graciously enough, but with more firmness on his piggy face than I'd seen since he rescued the child in the ring. "But for me it's late. And *tout franchement*, to be candid, I fear for my reputation" he smiled. "I have patients to see at seven and if I lack sleep and they see my fingers trembling I could lose whatever credit I've built up over ten years in this town."

We rise, with as much physical grace as we can muster. Despite the finality on ODG's face, a fresh impetus intervenes as we make our way into the corridor leading to the front door of the apartment.

"You're limping," du Greffand remarks.

"Very observant of you," I say, genuinely surprised. "It's only a surface cut and I can scarcely feel it."

"Permit me to take a look."

Before I can protest, the man pushes me firmly past the front door and into a small office. ODG is no longer the host but a man issuing orders with the brisk calm of the general practitioner.

"*Asseyez-vous.*"

When I'm sitting, du Greffand kneels and rolls up my trouser leg to expose my calf and the long, teasing cut. I glance over his shoulder and can see no sign of his wife in the corridor. Kindly, brusque, du Greffand waves away my protests, fetches a basin, tissues and bottles, cleans the cut and disinfects it, and wraps it in a crêpe bandage.

Looking down at my hands and the finger-nails I haven't been trimming quite as carefully as usual, the better to better to bear out my farmer identity, a moment comes back to me from a dream I'd had in the early morning hours. In it, a female voice was pointing out that I needed to attend to my fingernails, and in the dream my reaction was been that my fingernails were quite presentable, until I realized that I was a doctor and would need finely trimmed nails when dealing with my patients (in my dream they were children). The thought that my dreaming self took Olivier's place, as a doctor, distracts me for a moment.

I could kill him right here, I realize, where he kneels so solicitously over my leg. At any rate I could stun him with any of half a dozen implements to hand, and finish the job in a variety of unpleasant ways. And the wife? I have no desire to kill her too. In any case, old Fernande has seen and served me here at dinner, and would I be able to lie low for long enough to arrange for a Lysander to come and fetch me? (And land where? Was there a single spot in the sloping Garçonnier pastures where a Lizzie could land?) I have left a trail to *Oncle* Albert's. Besides these considerations, it would be a messy business and this isn't how I want to do it.

For all my bold talk in my head about my natural affinity for assassination, I'm not enjoying thinking about how I could kill my man, while his head is bowed in care, dabbing so delicately at my cut.

A bit of steely resolve is going to be necessary, in due course. Meanwhile I should use this opportunity, I know, to tease out any further confirmation I can.

"I must apologize," I say in a low, urgent voice, "for my words earlier. Hitler and all that. You might suppose I'd drunk too much. And I have." Du Greffand is trying to assure me of something, *je vous assure, monsieur*. I keep going nonetheless, and bend low, my head above his. "But the truth is that such views are a disguise I've adopted. A disguise which is very far from my own position. It suits me to use it as a way to deflect suspicion. In fact, I was hoping that while I'm here in the region I might be able to contact friends of precisely the opposite viewpoint. Friends willing to——"

But du Greffand doesn't even let me incriminate myself further.

"I wish you luck," he puts in. "Sincerely. But I wouldn't know how to direct you. All I know about our townspeople is their diseases. There," he adds, attempting now to pin the crêpe bandage to itself, careful not to include my flesh. "Hold still just one more moment."

The moment goes on and on. Something in the tone of his words has made me lose all interest in pressing him further. Frankly, *tout franchement*, he sounds as if he is speaking the truth, and I'm simply sitting here in the tiny study of a country doctor's apartment, in a French provincial town, and this good, solicitous man is seeing to my wounds, and that's all there is to it.

I'm in a dream, distracted, as du Greffand stands up and taps me on the shoulder. He has pulled down my trouser leg and I can feel a pleasant tightness in my calf. *"C'est tout fait,"* it's done, he says lightly, even charmingly. I stumble out my thanks as he walks off with the basin and unused tissues, and get unsteadily to my feet.

As I emerge into the corridor, dizzy with Armagnac and sudden movement, I'm amazed to find myself face to face with Hélène, who has seemingly been waiting there for me to come out of her husband's study and who leans in so close to me that I can't even see the mouth that has fascinated me all through the evening. She speaks in a whisper, her dark eyes——which are all I can see of her face, she's so close——dancing in their own light.

"Demain trois heures," she gabbles, seemingly as if we might be interrupted and she needs to get across the most important part of what she has to say.

Tomorrow three o'clock? For what? I'm quite drunk, I realize. And I'm racking my mind to remember whether some arrangement had been made for the morrow. But to do what?

"Où ça?" Where? I mumble, stupidly, hoping for a clue which will release the memory.

I see her stifle a giggle. What have I said that's funny?

"We can talk about *Mein Kampf*," she says, struggling to keep her voice down. "I've been waiting for so long for someone in this dreadful backwater," *dans cet arrière-pays de cauchemar*, this nightmare hinterland, is what she says, "who knows and loves the *Führer*'s work."

I realize I'm nodding. But still trying to think. Talk about *Mein Kampf*? Here, does she mean?

She reads my thoughts. "He'll be in the office in the Rue Magalit, until five. Press the bell downstairs. I'll let you in. *Trois heures.*"

For an awful moment I think she is going to blow me a kiss, but du Greffand reappears in the corridor, working his dry, clean hands together, and the kiss remains unexploded on the pinkish centre of her purple lips, like a puff of the bubble-gum to which GIs have been addicting our children.

8. *Hélène*

MORE PRESS-UPS, THE FOLLOWING MORNING.
Hup-two, hup-three, hup-four, on the creaking upstairs
bedroom floor. A *lot* more press-ups, thinking about what
to do and whether to rendez-vous with Madame ODG.
And whether it might complicate things if I did not. And
how it would complicate things if I did, assuming that she
didn't really want to talk about *Mein Kampf* and that the
backlit sparkle in her eyes and the bubblegum pout said
what they had appeared to be saying. Unless that was all
Armagnac.

I kept reminding myself that there was little or
nothing to be said for making friends with your target (let
alone with his wife). And everything to be said for not
doing so, if you were going to kill him.

That wasn't quite true, though. By knowing du
Greffand personally (happily it was all *monsieurs* and
madames with them, no first names to create a queasy
intimacy with the doctor whenever I thought about him),
and by talking to his wife, it was likely that I would acquire
precious knowledge of ODG's movements. Perhaps even
decisive information as to where he might be going, out of
town, say, on a particular day, when he could conveniently
be ambushed.

The other matter, which I didn't want to dwell on but
which kept returning to mind, was the disparity between
du Greffand as described in the dossier, the early-fifties
former motorbike champion, who owned a house with a
basement, and du Greffand in the flesh, the apartment-

dwelling late-sixtyish pedestrian, wobbly even on a bicycle. Looked at from one angle, it was troubling. Looked at from another, it was a negligible disparity. These were the kind of errors that could creep into anybody's dossier. And compared to the identifying match of his unusual name and his profession, such errors were irrelevant. Weren't they?

As for his apparent imperviousness to politics, that would simply be a well-established disguise. Why should he drop his mask for a total stranger like the Garçonnier fellow I was supposed to be?

I tried to put my worries to rest. After all, I had a job to do, one that lay clearly before me, namely to kill Dr Olivier du Greffand, and my role was simply to do it, not to compose a critique of his SOE dossier and its inadequacies.

Something was bothering me nonetheless, and it took me a while to work out what exactly it was. I liked the fellow. Not since my childhood had I met a Frenchman I actually liked. In my adult experience they were a preening, disputatious and treacherous crew, to the last man. The women were probably just as treacherous, but until now I'd steered clear. Du Greffand was neither vain nor disputatious. In fact he was the least argumentative person I think I'd ever come across. He was positively English in his civility, and I hadn't counted on that. Yet again, to clear this fresh irrelevance from my mind, I superimposed on ODG's affable piggyface the horrors of Marie Marquand under torture. It wasn't easy, since they refused to live in the same frame.

Also: what to communicate to base? Not about Hélène, which was none of their business at this point. (In my head I'd already started calling her Hélène rather than Madame du Greffand, a ridiculously grand appellation which didn't fit her morose flirtatiousness, so it was too late to preserve formalities.) But what to say about Olivier himself?

Nothing was surely the best.

I hadn't signaled my safe arrival yet, so although I loathed the radio set as much as we all did (especially since it so frequently led to our arrest and even cost us our lives), some communication was required.

Walking home the night before, after *dîner chez* du Greffand, in a glorious drunken swoon, in the dark, I had refrained from thoughts of cranking up the old radio when I reached Albert's. Last thing any field operative should do——send a message drunk. It wouldn't be the first time, but it was inadvisable. Morse code when drunk was harder than walking straight, which I was barely doing on the road to Labaronnerie.

Now, around midday on Monday, I pulled myself together and set up the wretched machine. I'd opened the suitcase lid the first night, to check that all the tubes had survived my landing in the Garçonnier pasture, and they had. Soon I was beeping away into the ether, summoning as always images of eager German tracking station operatives hurrying to try and zero in on the transmission source. Half an hour was what we were told we had before they traced us, but few liked to push it close to that limit.

When to the sessions of sweet silent thought…

I worked through it, encoding my message, and turned at last to the set, to tap in:

ywcstyordpnsdmpterpofpmfn

Or, when decoded:

targetfoundgumreconfirmid

Gum was my 'all-clear' codeword, to be inserted in every transmission. After a pause, the answer came.

egtwpybufgg

85

This decoded as *cleartokill*.
Once more I sent:
sdmctadtkypterpofpmfn
Gum request reconfirm id.
Then I shut down.

IT WAS RAINING as I headed for town and three o'clock Hitler-talk, drizzling gently but persistently enough to have soaked me by the time I reached the du Greffands, if it wasn't for one of several *imperméables* left behind by Albert's sons, waterproof windcheaters with deep, almost ecclesiastical hoods, loaned to me by the old man.

The hood renders me almost unidentifiable to passers-by. Gradually I realize that I am expecting enemy activity on the road in some form, troop carriers or jeeps or officers in limousines. Yet during the one and a half hour's walk from Labaronnerie not one such vehicle passes in either direction. When will it come, my first opportunity to test my Garçonnier papers and identity, for the first time? I've been tense with anticipation, yet as I reach the town I understand that I am confusing this region with the Tarn and its steady movement of German forces, quick to stop and interrogate stray French males of military age. It kept you on your toes.

Again I feel the strange pull of this untroubled countryside, inviting me to imagine that there really is no war, or only in the minds of its participants. Elsewhere, which is where I am now, there is no war and never has been. And you can live here, if you wish. Or, if you must, carry out your business without being disturbed, and be gone.

There it is, the lonely gutter-fed tree, up there, high on the house, under the eaves. I'm in the right street.

Rain descends the grey-yellow-greenish walls in slow sheets, like the shadows of strange creatures astride the roofs. No-one in the streets. Enormous shiny cobblestones, glistening, deformed but wedged together like an army of sleeping tortoises. I stay close to the walls until I reach the doorway with its glass and wrought iron.

I see myself walking up the wide spiral staircase that winds around the motionless *ascenseur*. Trying to stop myself from hurrying. From bounding. Because what if I'm bounding towards a scholarly discussion of *Mein Kampf*? And what if I'm not? The woman's old enough to be my mother and as vulgar as a Blackpool landlady, only French.

I see myself as I reach the apartment, heart pounding. The door opens, as in a dream, as I reach out to knock on it.

She's waiting for me behind the door. In a bathrobe. I barely have time to breathe in the apartment-smell of furniture polish overlaid with enough French perfume to fell an ox. One glance of confirmation and she throws herself against me, ignoring my dripping *imperméable*. In the old French fashion she is both elaborately made up and completely naked under the robe. We exchange not a single word about Hitler.

LACY, FRILLY BEDROOM, le boudoir de Madame Hélène. Now mingled with sharp scents of sweat, her perfume still saturates the room. I love every iota of its heavy furniture. I love the antimacassars and the beaded, faintly bohemian fringe (to be truthful, it's the only bohemian item in the room) on the overhead lampshade. Everything is so quiet now that I can tell it's still raining by the sound of overloaded gutters dripping in the street. How sweetly alive everything is!

I lie exhausted in Hélène's bed, amazed that such sensations and such feelings can exist in the world. I don't even know yet how deeply happy I am because the thought is too alarming to admit. I only know that sex is stranger than I have ever understood.

I don't, even now as I see her peeping at me from around the open bathroom door, find her especially attractive. But we mated, we conjugated, we fucked——as I have never known fucking before. Why? Why so? What on earth made it so tumultuous? Her body was a furnace, it's true, compared to which every girl I've known since Trudy was relatively tepid, no matter how willing. (And, Trudy dear, what did I know at 12 except that you were a Christmas decoration angel made miraculous flesh?) But that's not it.

She wanted to suck the very life out of me, certainly, and I thought I was acquainted with female appetite but I'd never come across anything so voracious before. It took every ounce of steel, every ounce of aggression I had (and I blessed all the shafts of tension that our circumstances lent to my last-ditch, last-fuck pistoning) to match her, meet her thrusts and master them. But that's not it either.

There was nothing strange about that aspect of it. It was just more animalistic than I'd experienced before.

No, I was wallowing in a completely new medium, and if you'd told me it was love I'd have laughed in your face. I'd have laughed wholeheartedly. Love, with a mad old Hitler-loving French bag pushing fifty, that I'd met only a few hours earlier?

It was like some hot oil I'd plunged into, and I'm not thinking now of her body, which was certainly slick and receptive as an oil well, and gushed like a broken pump. What I mean is my heart——my soul had plunged into a deep roaring pit of emotion that enlarged the whole world. It was luscious, this pit, and bottomless and infinitely supple and in it all boundaries broke and ceased, and time and death had no dominion. I wanted to go back there at once and I never wanted to go back there, because how could you hold still in everyday reality when you knew that however poor and cramped you were in mind and body there was a place where you were a giant, a Titan, riding the wind and ridden, in your turn, by eternity itself? A place where you were buggered by eternity itself, which became yours to spray into the pit, into this hole, this nest, this cavern that transmuted everything into glory. A place of absolute certainty. A place of freedom, that was what it was, of freedom.

And all this in the bed of a poor frustrated housewife in provincial France, putting frantic horns on her ageing, overworked husband, and fucking (crying and grunting *Oui! Oui! Oui!* over and over like the last little piggy in all the world) with what must truly have been the fear that it was the final go-round for unbridled passion——this was freedom?

Of course I knew what it was. I didn't have to be told, to go to a book or a doctor or a smart, sneering pal to be reminded that if there was one thing my soul sought (and avoided) to make it complete, it was the 'real' mother my childhood had kept in abeyance till I was 12, and then delivered in a false, disappointing form. In Edie-form. I never wanted to court that disappointment again. I'd never even slept with a girl six months older than I was, let alone 20 years older, like Hélène.

I can tell you, though, from (as they say) personal experience, that if you ever catch up with your past——with that hidden treasure you've been chasing all your life whether you know it or not——it's a mind-fuck to beat anything you've ever known. What I poured into Hélène was every last withheld ounce of undeclared longing, every refusal to mourn, every clenched nerve, twenty-eight years of waiting. God knows what she thought *she* was getting. Maybe all French farmers have up their sleeve as ferocious a performance as I delivered that afternoon. She was my permission to let it rip at last, and I felt every seam break in the bandage of denial that I'd wound around my whole life, day after day, after week, after year. I burst through like a snake out of a skin ten sizes too small. Towards the end even her ravenous eyes, that said fuck me to the ends of the earth, to the ends of time, began to stare in awe and distantly rising anxiety. What had she unleashed? The minotaur?

It was the signal I needed. I needed to see fear, a hint of fear, to make my demonic ride, my return——my Runt's Revenge——complete. There was still the why-so-long, why did you make me wait so long? There was still anger, and there had to be punishment mixed in with the unearthly joy.

No wonder she's peeping at me round the bathroom door as I lie here, sprawled on the bed, harmless as my limp, shriveled cock. Her eyes are a little stunned, and her bruised mouth lacks all calculation. It's the first time I've seen her mouth without its performance. To judge by her expression poor Hélène, is thinking: I knew I'd been missing the most explosive part of my life, but it seems to me now that I've been missing even more than I knew. Is this what true men are? Demons when roused? Bulls? More than bulls, though, because what she saw in my eyes was a devouring that went beyond strength, beyond lust. (It was time I was feasting on, but she couldn't know that. I was ripping the sinew from the bad, taut years, with my teeth.)

It's time to go. I could walk back to Labaronnerie naked without a second thought. Face, for that matter, a firing squad naked.

I've never known what it was to have every corner of my spirit cleansed, every cobweb found and cast out. All *comptes* quit. What do I mean? All accounts balanced. Not a debt to pay in any crevice of my soul. I'm done, sorted. The expression, 'cleaned my clock,' surges weirdly to mind, although that usually refers to a savage beating. But it is in fact my *clock*, my waste of years, that has just been cleaned. My *past*, my *waste*. *Now* I understood why Shakespeare rhymed those two words!

It might be better to die now. Because when will I ever again feel so quit, so quitted and acquitted? So ready?

"You want the bathroom?" my saviour asks timidly from the doorway of the *salle de bain*.

I shake my head.

Did I shake my head?

Truthfully I'm on another planet. And I don't think I want to wash an iota of stink or sweat off my sanctified body.

BUT WHAT IN God's name was I doing? The shock of it came to me before I'd even got out of the apartment, and it swept me so completely off my horse that I started running, thoughtless, down the spiral stairs in jacket and trousers and without my raincoat, and had to turn and scurry back up two floors and knock on the door to find Hélène convinced I must have come back for another quick one. Then to disentangle myself, find the guilty *imperméable* (*Ça t'appartient, ma chérie?* Whose the hell is this, dear?), lying crumpled on the floor in the darkling corridor where I'd flung it, and hurry back into the stairwell.

Thinking, *What in God's name am I doing?*

If there was an assassin's handbook, a *Guide Bleu* to Killing Without Complications, lesson one was surely, Do not be dallying with your target's spouse, and above all, *surtout*, of all places not in your target's bedroom.

But as soon as I was out of the house, down the street and away into the trailing little roads of miniature suburbia, villas with their neatly trimmed fruit trees and their tidy dreary house-fronts, I lifted my face to the rain spattering down on my head (to hell with the cavernous raincoat hood). Once more I basked and gloried. The joy was in my veins, my blood, my body, and there was a distillation of this feeling, in my head, that I carried with me now like a key or a code. And when——

Wait——

When to the sessions of sweet silent thought....

I rattled through my sonnet, flushed with the thought that I had let two hours and more go by without a precautionary recitation. It was all still there. It was there, and not all the bandage-bursting or the bedroom-jungle romps with Hélène could dislodge it, *Dieu merci*.

Yet when——this had been my thought——when they stood me against a wall (that old brick wall bruised and chipped with bullet-holes against which, in imagination, Marie Marquand had met her end), I had a place to go now, in my head. Long before then, too, sitting in the cell waiting for the guards to come and take me to my firing squad appointment, I could turn the key, whisper the codeword, *Hélène,* and open a world that was mine alone and that was larger and more vivid than any present torture chamber on earth.

When to the sessions of sweet silent thought indeed! I'm dripping wet when I reach Labaronnerie and hurry to the stairs hoping to reach my bed and lie and relive every moment of the afternoon, in sessions of sweet silent thought. Instead *Monsieur! Monsieur!* comes old Albert's voice with its mandolin twang.

There's news.

Dr du Greffand has phoned for me.

As I stand there frozen, thinking the worst but unable to give it form, Albert adds that the doctor wanted to know if I desired to go fishing with him tonight.

Fishing?

Fishing, Albert repeats and, to clear my leaden foreigner's head, mimes casting a miniature rod. Fishing. It would be a good night for *la pêche,* Albert continues, with the river high but still sluggish, before the water comes down off the mountains. The doctor will come by this evening, en route to the river. If *Monsieur* requires a bicycle, there are several in the shed. Fishing rods are also in the shed. Albert eyes me as if to say, You have been warned, before turning away as he speaks. The doctor, Albert says, is said by all to be an able fisherman.

Jolting awake from visions of a showdown stage-managed by a furious, humiliated du Greffand——two men go out on bicycles, only one returns——who has come home to find his apartment reeking of erotic mayhem and has tortured my name out of Hélène (using the water torture, as practised on Marie by ODG himself), I ask Albert when it was that *le docteur* had phoned. *Vers deux heures,* around two, the old man says. He, Albert, was eating his bread, his *peng* (that mandolin twang again, converting *pain* to *peng*) and cheese, when the phone rang.

So not a vengeful du Greffand rendez-vous, not at innocent two p.m., a hundred years ago, while I was trudging into town.

Only then, as I thank Albert and continue up the stairs, does it come to me what a perfect scenario a fishing expedition is, if not for Dr du Greffand then for me.

Two men go fishing in the flushed, soon-to-be-rushing river, swollen with rain. Neither returns. Body of one found floating, at last. The *pauv' docteur*, an able fisherman, *bien sûr*, but powerless before the deluge from the mountains. The other, a visitor to the region, unwary, presumed swept away to the sea, or trapped under rocks, a bluish-pale albino manatee, nibbled by crabs.

In this vision I see my own dead body more clearly than I see ODG's.

9. *Learning to fish*

ET ALORS? *ASKS THE GOOD DOCTOR.*
Well then? His round cheeks are red with the effort of
cycling through the drizzle, his eyes aglow with
exercise——I can see his excitement even in the dark,
flagstoned lobby of Labaronnerie——and the delicious
prospect of casting a midnight fly. *On va à la pêche?* A-
fishing we shall go?

What a nice fellow. On his return home at 5:30
prompt, he finds his wife quietly reading as usual, *comme
d'habitude.* Unless a patient detains him, Hélène has
mentioned, he's home by 5:45, certainly no earlier. The
meal is prepared, the wine awaits (they will drink it
watered, I feel sure). The apartment is a little cooler than
he expected, perhaps, after Hélène's labours of ventilation,
making sure all trace of our riot is gone.

Stop this, I tell myself. Absurd that when I should be
plotting murder, I'm reduced to the preoccupations of a
common adulterer!

A-fishing we shall go. I had not forgotten, after the
Sunday evening meal chez du Greffand, that during the
meal there was a mention of ODG using his bicycle to go
fishing. My guess, at the time, was that the fishing trips
were the cover for the fellow's espionage work. After he
ignored the lure I dangled before him in his study, when I
spoke of hoping to meet up with local people inimical to
Hitler, I never expected to be invited to join him on an
angling expedition, real or otherwise.

Fishing, or what I took to be 'fishing,' would be a first-rate cover. Indeed, how else might a busy country doctor manage to disappear from view so frequently, and so completely? Hunting would do the trick, but it involves guns and evokes violence. Fishing has a peaceful, random aura. Purposeless, almost. (I had been fishing exactly once in my life, on holiday with Harry and Edie, and that had been thoroughly purposeless.) Also interesting was the way the subject had come up, over supper, a propos du Greffand's lack of need for petrol vouchers and the uses to which he put his bicycle. It needn't have come up at all; fishing, in other words, was an activity ODG had no call to mention in front of his wife if she knew it hid a different kind of sport, so my hypothesis assumed that Hélène knew nothing of ODG's double or indeed triple life of doctor, SOE agent, and Nazi counterspy. It was a plausible assumption, it seemed to me. While I had to believe that the smiling porcine doctor was a practised liar, Hélène was a different type of human being altogether. Self-dramatizing, certainly; but she was so transparently full of her woes that I couldn't picture her as a convincing actress.

This had been my first estimate of her, at any rate. Now, to judge from her husband's happy demeanour as we set out for the river, wobbling along on our bicycles with our fishing tackle balanced on the handlebars, Hélène had found a bit of acting talent, or at least the gumption to keep mum about our afternoon romp.

It was time to put Hélène out of my mind.

Unfortunately, du Greffand's very presence, his burbling chatter as we cycled slowly down the road, kept bringing her back to mind. He was yakking on about flies and lines and different fishing rods and I had no idea what he was talking about. I could only tell that he was in his element.

And I? What element was I in? I'd slept with married women before. Not often, but a couple of times at least. What I'd never done was go fishing——or engage in any social activity whatsoever——with the husband.

Were we in fact, ODG and I, going fishing (as opposed to going 'fishing')? Everything suggested we were. We had the equipment, and fishing was all du Greffand was talking about, the perch and trout and salmon he'd caught, their weight and number and the time it had taken to exhaust them and bring them to the shallows. But I kept thinking it was a ruse. All evening, indeed, as we unpacked our gear and settled in to fish, I expected footsteps behind us, or the silent appearance at the treeline of companions who hadn't bothered with the charade of fishing rods and baskets full of bait. "Let me introduce you to some friends," ODG would say.

Instead night came on steadily, and it was still only the two of us. For a long while we were shrouded in darkness, with only the sounds of the woods around us, and the faint slap of our lures as we fished and the tiny water-gasps of fish rising. Then du Greffand lit a hurricane lamp and I was conscious once more of expecting company, drawn by the light. No-one arrived, and finally ODG led me, with the lamp showing the way, into undergrowth beside the shore, where he kept a small, flat-bottomed boat. We dragged it down to the water, clambered in with our baskets and rods, and floated out onto the calm of the river's wide, peaceful elbow, to fish in solitary state, by moonlight.

There was a kind of rapture to it, I must admit. As I say, I'd only ever been fishing the once, with Harry, when he and I and Edie went to the South Coast and we rented the rods and the bait and fished unsuccessfully off a pier. I had to admit to du Greffand that I didn't know the first thing about fishing, as he could tell when I tried to assemble my fishing rod. It must have seemed strange to him that a Garçonnier knew nothing of so universal a country practice, but I explained that I was a city Garçonnier and not the country mouse variety. This confession was to stand me in good stead later that night, but also, in another way, in disastrous stead.

We began our stint at a broad, sharply winding bend between forested shorelines, where the dark line of distant shore showed the river bulging to the dimensions of a small lake. There was light enough, when we arrived, to see the rough water in the middle, water in a hurry and rippling at speed. Around it smoother areas swirled like idle shoppers looking for a place to rest, and at the edges, especially at the elbow of the bend, where we were, stood rock-lined pools where the water slowed contemplatively, heading nowhere.

ODG set about teaching me everything about the fishing game, or at least everything you could teach a duffer in a single night, with exemplary patience. He also had a sense of humour, something I'd found sadly lacking in his countrymen until now. This came in handy as I periodically stabbed myself, and him, with my hook. Gathering darkness is far from the ideal hour for learning how to cast, and there were times when neither of us were quite sure, until I reeled in after a practice cast, whether my hook was in the water or somewhere behind us on a branch. But ODG put up with this, treating me with unfailing courtesy. He really was a good sport——I must have been ruining what would have been a perfect evening's fishing if his companion had known how to fish, a reward for fretful hours spent with ailing, often difficult patients.

No doubt he'd pictured us standing there in utter calm, each of us casting his line and casting again and slowly reeling in, in what after a few hours of it I discovered to be the most sweetly soporific rhythm in the world. But I had to be rescued from my own clumsiness every two minutes, and once more shown how to bait my hook and how to flick my line out across the stream. When I watched him do it, this fat little fellow who wobbled on a bicycle and seemed to lack all natural grace, I saw a magical transformation. In his hand the rod was as precise as an orchestral conductor's wand instructing the strings or quickly, lightly bringing in the woodwinds with a flick of the baton. He himself hardly seemed to move at all, and his squat form and stubby torso seemed to anchor him and allow the line to fly mazily over the water as if it were his own true spirit expressing itself, free of his bulky, accidental body. The line flew out a folded thing, almost like a chain of insects, a squadron of suicidal gnats in close formation, one behind the other, before unleashing itself, uncurling into a single filament, a tiny arm stretching as if to pluck an equally small, floating petal from the surface of the stream forty feet away. The beauty of it was that the fishing line didn't seem alien to the scene as it flashed over the water, as a gun does, or as a bullet even while it travels, with its vile imperious noise. Like an arrow in its sinew-sound, the line unreeling made a companionable hum, and the dark line hovering over the water continued to evoke, for me, the path taken by a hurrying fly as it raced out in search of a mouth to tempt.

Then darkness finally ate up our view of the process, and we resorted to what I've later learned to call topwater bait, little jitterbug devices that wriggle on the surface and attract the fish by sound, not sight. In the dark this too acquired a magic, as if we were truly conjurors, witches who could summon tiny rattling, splashing creatures, at our command, to deceive our prey. To the atavistic sensation that hunting brings, filling the mind with an intentness as old as predatory life itself, was added a delicate play of trickery and disguise. Each cast was like the repetitive questioning of a bird call, content to keep on trying until it met with an answer. What a devious, clever creature man was, I couldn't help thinking as we sat at last in du Greffand's little boat and revelled, now that the rain had ceased and the clouds had blown away, in the moonlight on the peaceful river elbow, yes, funny little awkward monkey that we were, flatfooted, slow, inelegant——but how resourceful! Floating in midstream on a piece of sculpted wood, while the pooling water spun us slowly round, the cunning of our hands and brain had enabled us to manufacture rod and line and lure so witty and exact that we were able to pretend we were a waterfly, a tiny insect boatman or flailing, drowning moth. Extraordinary creature that man was! And strange philosophical activity that fishing was! I could never have guessed this, sitting bored to death on the bait-stinking pier in Hove, next to poor huge frustrated sweating Harry who'd been so eager to play surrogate father and enable me to catch my first fish.

But here, at night, on water, amid the soft intermittent plops of water-splash and bird cries and the brief sounds of triumph, from the shore, made by nocturnal hunters with methods simpler than ours, it was all philosophy. We were the squat little mole of leisure, we in our drying *imperméables*, who delegated the hard work, via our hands, to our fishing line, and sat in contemplation of the universe. Wasn't this how man had become man? By sheer surplus? Once the hunters had hunted and the gatherers had gathered, plenty of time was left. We had a choice. Should we sleep the gift of time away like cats and dogs or, instead, sit awake and look and listen and seek to understand? Whatever there was to understand in the bowl of universe where we sat, ODG and I, where we floated, it was there all around us, available, unpacked for our inspection. Cries, the silky night itself with its soft sweet-smelling air cleansed by the long rain; water, that strange dense yet ever-flexing medium; and the countless inhabitants of the planets from the predators (ourselves included) who now emerged to feed in concert with their prey, right down to the insects joyously released by the end of the downpour. They were humming around us mockingly, like wild fish food, nature's free sample, on offer while stocks lasted and without the steel hook that turned our baited simulacra into death traps.

We were afloat, it seemed to me, on a symphony of little sounds and premises for contemplation. Never had I felt the mind more isolated and alert and prompted, I felt, by the teeming vividness of life: here you are, it seemed to say, afloat in your own diorama, with the world laid out around you. Now; try and *get* it, now; if you can't get it now, when will you get it?

BEFORE WE REACHED this oasis of silence, each of us wrapped up in and satisfied by our own listening to and sensing of the nighttime world, black-cloaked and challenging us to unmask it, there had been a good deal of conversation, some of it technical, to do with fishing, some of it trivial, some of it astonishingly intimate.

He was an easy man to relax with, this ODG. Some people have the knack; I don't know what it is; others mean well in every possible way but you can no more relax in their company than you could during a police interrogation. They do all the right things, these unrelaxing people, but perhaps their problem is that they themselves don't know how to relax, and their solicitousness drives you crazy.

He was comfortable company even when he talked about what for me were unrelaxing matters, such as his wife. He talked about Hélène a lot. Clearly she was always on his mind. As absurd as it was——what right did I have to any such feelings?——I liked him terribly for the way he spoke about her, with love and tender courtesy, yet candidly and without condescension. Without unkindness either. This was a man impossible to dislike. But I was already wounding him behind his back and, since he was the one and only Olivier du Greffand, the man who somehow (where did he find the time?) worked both ends of the undercover game against the middle and had betrayed Marie Marquand to her death, I was going to have to kill him, this likeable fellow who was teaching me so patiently how to fish. There was no way out of it that I could see. I would simply have to kill him and that's all there was to it.

But why should it have to be tonight? Did I *have* to do it tonight?

I discovered that he was a good teacher, the old *docteur*. The right sort of teacher, not in too much of a hurry for you to get it all right at once. Besides, I think I knew as well as he did that to learn to cast a fishing line really well was not an evening's work, no matter how well co-ordinated you were. And there was more involved than mastery of rod and line, much more. Ultimately, I realized, any fool could toss the bait out forty feet. The art lay in learning to think like a fish, to feel, as you played the hunter's part, flicking your rod out across the water, that you were also the creature in the mirror, that you were the fish itself gazing up from beneath the glass. You were both; you were you *and* the fish, hunter and prey, and at the instant when you truly inhabited both parties the line would tauten, and the filament connecting you would find its mark and make connection and you'd reel in your double, your alter ego, until you held it in your hands.

Then you could dislodge the barb that joined you and release your very self——farewell, brother——out of your medium and back into his.

Philosophical! That's what it was. You spent your lifetime fishing for your double in the mirror of existence, and now, afloat on midnight water, you reached deep into the darkness and felt an answering tug at last, and slowly, slowly, with infinite care, reeling in and holding and releasing a little and reeling in again, an Orpheus afraid that at any instant his Eurydice will slip out of his hand and vanish into Pluto's maw, you bring your dark twin to the light.

What you do not do, not if you can possibly avoid it, if you are Dr Olivier du Greffand and Runt Rawlinson, disguised as Jean-Louis Garçonnier, sharing a little flat-bottomed boat going round in slow pooling circles in the elbow of a river at midnight, is think about the baited hook and line that connects the two of you.

Because who is playing whom?

Am I also fishing for ODG and a word, a casual phrase even, that will confirm his duplicitous existence? I am. And my bait, in place of wriggling jitterbug lures, consists of jiggling watertop ploys of conversation, as I trail this or that harmless-seeming topic before his quiet, goggling fish-eyes. He rises to none. Or rather, he rises to them all, friendly soul that he is, nuzzles them, delicately and apparently effortlessly removes the matter from the steel trap within it, and munches affably, before my baffled gaze.

So does this mean that he is somehow innocent (but he *is* Dr Olivier du Greffand, damn it!)? Or that to understand the scene you must see it in a mirror: is he in fact playing *me* like a fish, inducing me to stumble onto the alluring bait of his pretended ignorance of all matters political, let alone conspiratorial, and over and over again hauling me gasping into the air, to land slap in his bucket of dupes?

Better not to think of this (just as it's better not to think of Hélène, if possible *not at all*, not once, all night). Better to fish.

Better also not to wonder whether beneath ODG's utterly convincing persona, fond friendly piggy-ODG snuffling at my side, might lie not only a triple agent but also (and this will be child's play if you're already a counterspy in a murderous world) a husband who knows all about you and his wife, and is waiting, all appearances to the contrary, to gut you like a trout.

Surely not.

But why not? If you're the dark secret spy and torturer ODG, and no sooner have you returned home than you sniff out your wife's whole game, wouldn't you press home your revenge in just this manner? A friendly invitation to midnight sport *à deux*, far from prying eyes; a mask of affable civility; and then the knife in the guts. After all, if you can convince both sides in a deadly global conflict that you work for them and them alone, when you're actually betraying them both right left and centre, you're in your groove. All you have to do is maintain your seamless impersonation of a harmless old buffer.

And if you're such an accomplished superspy, how would you not have sniffed out the change in your apartment? The *change*? Dear God, the place was another universe, for me at least, after that tumultuous afternoon fuck. I could hardly recognize it as the drab provincial hole it had been a few minutes before, with its tired *ancien régime* furnishings. Afterwards, the whole place was irradiated with gratified desire. It glowed, it was radioactive. Every piece of frippery, and not just the overhead lampshade in the bedroom, now sported a beaded fringe as if our lust had coagulated into drops of amber everywhere you turned. How in God's name could du Greffand not have noticed any of this when he returned home? He'd left the place a French mausoleum and come back to a brothel in New Orleans. And no matter how much airing and perfume-spraying Hélène had accomplished, wouldn't it have immediately struck a practised spy as suspiciously *too much*?

Besides which, mightn't she have simply flung herself weeping into her husband's arms, confessing all? Stranger things happen.

And now of course he would be waiting for *le moment propice*, the right moment, to kill me, while enjoying the dalliance, plump cat toying with runt-mouse.

Better not to think about such things, but just to fish.

And the final thing that it was best not to think about, of course, was that with every hour that passed on the silent midnight shore, just the two of us, and then later afloat on the rising flood where killing him and disposing of the body would be even easier and quicker than on shore, I was letting slip a golden opportunity to finish my own job. When might such a perfect opportunity recur (not only in this instance, on this mission, but in my life generally or indeed in the life of any assassin)? How often could you expect to find yourself cloistered in darkness with an unsuspecting victim, beside a rushing river with no-one to see or hear a thing?

But as long as I had doubts; and until London answered my reconfirmation query——

And the fact remained: once I'd done the deed, there would be no more radioactive encounters with Hélène, ever again.

Better just to keep fishing.

IT IS MANY hours before I catch my first fish——my very first fish ever, since neither Harry nor I caught a single one in Hove, and Edie sat chortling with amusement every time we reeled in excitedly to reveal a little sodden mass of seaweed at the end of our line.

By then, when my first fish takes the bait, it's dark and I feel as if this has helped. The poor impatient creature couldn't see that it was Duffer Garçonnier for whose artless cast it fell. Under cover of night I've succeeded in impersonating a real fisherman. I feel like Nimrod the mighty hunter as I hold the wriggling fish up to the moon, like Jason holding aloft the Golden Fleece.

Du Greffand has by now netted more than a dozen, and neither gloried gloatingly over them and made me feel small, nor shrugged off his successes, which would have made me feel smaller still.

Our conversation, too, has progressed from fishing stories to childhood tales more generally.

"Fishing was my escape," ODG tells me, "of course not fishing like this with expensive equipment but fishing with a home-made fishing pole and worms and often maggots, which were not so hard to find for yourself. Close to where I lived were some kennels and if you could steal a piece of rotting meat that was meant for the dogs, you would soon have plenty of maggots. My first great friend, Christian, was mad for fishing and I went with him, first to have his company because he was great for stories and jokes and having fun, and then because I enjoyed being so completely distracted by the fishing itself.

"My mother," he continued, "was fragile in health, perhaps all her life, as she herself maintained, but perhaps also to limit the attentions of my father, by which I mean, I'm afraid, what it sounds like. As an invalid she was able to refuse him favours which she did not want from him. This was difficult for him too, and in our household there was always tension. His demands, her refusal. His anger. He was a gendarme, a big man physically——as you can see, I take after my mother, who was small, but also thin. During my life I have asked myself whether I allow myself to be fat, which was not on either side of my family at all, because in this way I hope, unconsciously, to avoid becoming the invalid my mother was. Perhaps that sounds absurd to you, but to me it sometimes seems as if my body as it is, my girth, is a kind of investment or insurance against the perpetual illness I saw in my poor thin mother. And perhaps also against the anger I saw so often in my poor thin tall father. Fat people are often more peaceful in my opinion——I do not say this to my patients——and certainly the example I have from my childhood is a household of two thin angry people, the kind of household I would never want to live in again.

"It was in any case a long time before I married. I was nearly sixty years old and had decided that I was married to my work, very happily, and had no desire to take the risk of spending my later years in the atmosphere of tension which was all I knew of marriage, from my parents."

He was silent for a time. Fish, breaking the surface, hiccuped softly in the dark. The night was so tranquil now, and time so elastic as we cast and waited, reeled in and cast again, that it could have been five minutes or thirty before du Greffand spoke again.

"Perhaps I should have kept to my original resolve. You've met my wife, Jean-Louis. May I call you Jean-Louis? One may work beside a man, or eat and drink with him, or play cards with him for forty years without employing his first name. But for me, to fish beside someone is always to be fishing again beside my friend Christian. It is too companionable to remain only polite, friendly strangers.

"So," he said, "you have met my wife."

My trance was broken, and I was fishing with rather less relaxation now.

"I am not a psychiatrist," du Greffand continued, "but I can't help noticing that I have imitated my father by marrying a woman with a disappointed look in her eye. Was she always that way? Did she look disappointed already when I met her? I certainly don't remember it so, but it's possible that this look was precisely what I was searching for, without knowing it, because it was the look that reminded me of home. That sounds stupid, doesn't it? But isn't that how we choose our mate? What do you think?"

In the silence I was genuinely unable to think of an answer.

"Well, it's not fair of me to ask you, because I surmise that you are not married. Am I right?"

"Yes."

"I don't say this in order to prove myself an amateur psychic. I simply deduce from your presence here to help old Albert in his hour of need, that you did not have a family to persuade that this was a necessary absence from them. I hope you won't think me cynical, Jean-Louis, when I say that I believe few wives would gladly loan their husbands to an ageing old relative. Unless, of course——"a sudden thought tickled him, and he could hardly keep the amusement out of his voice, "——the wife was gambling on the possibility that *le bon Albert* having, poor man, already lost two sons to the war, might lose the other two and decide to settle Labaronnerie on you. Forgive me. I don't mean to speak heartlessly of your relatives, or of your putative wife. I take it she is imaginary?"

"She lives only in your imagination, Olivier," I said, faintly sickened to find how much I too wanted to express, by using his first name as he had mine, the strange, tender proximity of a night afloat, hour after hour, in darkness and congenial silence.

"Wise fellow. I don't mean to speak ill of Hélène. Perhaps she was indeed already a little disappointed when she met me. I hope I don't need to take the blame for every part of her discouraged spirit. She had seen and left behind her the youthful side of forty, she had lived in Paris and disported herself without finding a partner for life, and when her mother became, like mine had been, an invalid ——but a real one, without the added incentive for theatre that my mother felt she had——Hélène abandoned Paris to come home and look after her. And at the same time, perhaps, abandoned her hopes of a Parisian life with the Parisian husband she had never found. Time passes, and the mother is now dead. I was her doctor, and you will understand that this is how I met Hélène, the dutiful daughter. I had been the mother's doctor for many years, and had heard a good deal about the glamorous Parisian daughter, of whom *maman* was very proud. When I say the dutiful daughter, I don't mean to sound less than truly complimentary. I honoured Hélène, and still honour her greatly, both for returning to look after her mother——like me, she was an only child——and also for making such a tender and attentive job of her nursing.

"Have you noticed," said Olivier (and I've been dreading this moment, when I must redact honestly the move not only in our conversations but in my head, too, from du Greffand to Olivier), "how rarely only children marry only children? I have. No doubt we are looking for the larger family, the family enlarged by siblings, that we never had, and seeking it among those who are its products. But I, and she, sought out our like, our *semblable*, not our complementary other half. I don't know what your guess would be as to the reason for this," and I'm happy for him to continue without waiting for me to offer a guess, since I don't have one, "but I believe it is because we were both, in middle age, making our choice of a spouse when we ourselves possessed less hopeful illusions than a younger bride or bridegroom. The place that when we're young we keep open in our souls, the half of us we reserve for our perfect soulmate, we have long since sealed over by the time we reach the age that Hélène and I were on our marriage day. We have settled already, you might say, for ourselves as a self-sufficent entirety, and closed the door on our hopes of being completed by another. We have ourselves already become that other, and when two middle-aged people marry they bring to each other a finished world of hopes and habits. You must then align yourselves, side by side, instead of melting into one two-headed creature. In some ways the side-by-side life is easier, in other ways harder. Both require give and take, I think."

He falls silent again, and we fish in unbroken peace for a while before my companion——*Olivier*, damn it, and yet he's also still ODG, since ODG is the man I'm here to kill, the man I must kill if he *is* the ODG of my dossier——speaks again.

"It occurs to me that I spoke just now of my mother as though she only acted out her illness. I implied that it was chiefly theatre and I don't mean to give that impression. But my father was a violent man. I believe he was not always that way but that his life as a gendarme made opportunities for him to take out his frustrations in a physical way, on other people, instead of keeping them inside as we mostly do. So——I'm saying that my mother was able to find a further use for her illness. It's hard to hit and beat a person who is bedridden."

The emotion in his voice is so intense now that I want to interject, somehow, something of mine, to stem his monologue. I'm finding it hard being Jean-Louis Garçonnier, a man with no legitimate memories of his own.

"But let me return," he says quickly, "to what I meant to say about Hélène and myself, which was not said to embarrass you with confidences more intimate than even a fishing companion can expected to endure," once more, amusement tinges his voice, "but rather to ask a favour."

"Of course," I say, when at last I realize that the silence is not our soporific conversational rhythm reinstalling itself, but is Olivier waiting for an answer.

"Thank you. You see, Hélène has rightly no desire to sink into the tedium of *la vie de province*, provincial life, or to spend it with contemporaries of hers who have spent their whole life in the town and whose intellectual boundaries are correspondingly small, or with contemporaries of mine who are tiresome for the same reason and in addition are old men. Fresh, interesting company is hard to find. You have come into our life by a small miracle, if I may so describe the courage and physical skill with which you saved a complete stranger's life. You will not stay, I fear, for very long, although I would like to think that even when one of Albert's sons returns to relieve you from duty, and you depart, your stay with us will incline you to visit the town again. You will always find as warm a welcome with us as with your relatives at Labaronnerie."

Wherever this is going, I'm now praying for it to stop, and trying to think of some way to change the subject without seeming rude.

"What I'm trying to say, which perhaps in your natural sympathy and affinity for people you have already guessed, is that Hélène is lonely. I'm at work all day. She pines, not necessarily for me, but certainly for intelligent conversation. She sits and reads, but it makes her feel, as she says, a hundred years old, to spend all day reading. I have urged her to find a job, but..."

Abruptly I notice a little activity around Olivier's jigging bait. He has not seen it yet. My prayers intensify.

"After Paris," Olivier shakes his little piggy head, "she regards local life as a bad joke out of one of her books, and as precisely the kind of narrow gossipy world she wanted to get away from in the first place. I do not need to tell you that I wish for her sake that I had not detained her here, despite the joy she has given me. I mean I never would have wished for our marriage to become an imprisonment."

"Olivier," I interrupt, as the bubbles increase and his lure bobs briefly under the water.

"I'm asking you, dear friend," Olivier continues imperviously, since it is clearly costing him some effort of soul and some concentration to come out with the favour he mentioned, "if on such short acquaintance I may call you that, and surely when a man saves your life it renders that acquaintance as profound as many lifelong friendships can boast——"

"You've got a fish," I blurt, but he is launched on another trajectory entirely, and pays no attention.

"I'm asking you whether, if you have any time to spare from your merciful labours at Labaronnerie, and if you can persuade Albert to let you go from time to time——I'm asking you whether you mightn't visit Hélène and indulge her need for keen and pleasing talk——"

"A fish!" I cry. "You've got a fish, Olivier!"

And at last the distraction is achieved, and I am spared the challenge of accepting with a straight face my poor dear cuckolded new friend's request that I console his lonely wife.

Of course I am not a complete innocent; or a complete idiot. And as we together lure the newly snagged fish——and, precisely! who is the newly snagged one here, he or I?——towards the boat, I consider, not for the first time, the possibility that from our first evening together the rendez-vous with Mme du Greffand and the panting consummation and the whole amorous kit and caboodle have in fact been cooked up by Monsieur *and* Madame du Greffand for the pleasure of both; of all three of us, indeed. Part of that pleasure, for them (and presumably for me too) would be the illusion of an adultery, adding spice all round. The sordid alternative to this, namely open concubinage, an ageing doctor acting as his wife's pandar, would hardly make much fun for any of us. (I'm assuming that ODG's part of the fun is hearing the tales of an amorous adventure which would lack much of its spark if it weren't illicit, or seemingly so.) Yet once the fuse has been lit, as it already has, with some splendid opening fireworks accomplished into the bargain, why would the voyeur-husband now need to give me the key, in effect, to his apartment, himself? Why the further encouragement?

It begs some thought, as I watch Olivier play his fish and calmly let it run before hauling it back once more, letting it twist and dive and even leap, before drawing its yielding form to the boat. Perhaps, in this rather seamy version of our nascent *ménage à trois* (for which I have not the slightest evidence outside my naturally evil and suspicious mind), Monsieur and Madame have been hashing over the news of my magnificent overture with Madame this afternoon, and are simply keen that I should not take fright. They want the opera to continue, with as many arias, to judge by Olivier's enthusiasm, as I can fit in while I'm here.

But if this nasty scenario is accurate, I've no desire to play a part in it. What's more I don't want to think about it right now; I don't want to dwell at all on Hélène or her needs or their marriage, and I now need a fresh topic for conversation, as Olivier returns the glistening fish, unhooked and stroked and praised in all its silvery majesty, into the water beside the boat.

"But will you oblige me by visiting her?" Olivier insists.

"Of course," I say.

I find my fresh topic by deciding to borrow my own life. Why shouldn't Jean-Louis Garçonnier have had, just as Hélène did, a spell in Paris? Why not a childhood in the capital? I start to paint 1920s Montmartre for Olivier, and within its merry bohemianism my rootless, mercenary upbringing. My premise is that I too have known beginnings I've been seeking to forget, and grew up with a model of domesticity which has discouraged me, as Olivier's did, from settling too quickly into my own version.

I go so far as to place my Garçonnier childhood in and out of the Mon Chat Noir, as mine was (Hélène will enjoy these risqué tales, I hear Olivier thinking). To this day I wish I hadn't done so, because of what was to follow in the way of ODG's answering reminiscences.

As I progress, my imagination takes wing and my semi-fictional self discovers he is not a Garçonnier by blood, but only by name. In my account of my French upbringing, which moves me as much as if it were true, I am an adopted child, a foundling, orphaned in the deepest recesses of my soul.

And how eloquently ODG now speaks about the lifelong suffering of the orphan! He himself, though he can claim no such grudge against the world, has known what it feels like to feel no trace of kinship, in your spirit, with those who raise you. "We are forever seeking to atone, to apologize, Jean-Louis," he says, looking closely at me in the moonlight. I can only see his piggy, pouchy cheeks, not his eyes, but I feel that his stillness is now addressed to me, along with the intensity in his voice. "We still regard ourselves as guilty, although we have done nothing to earn our outcast fate. I ran away from home at 13, and I have no regrets about it. One more beating from my father and I might have turned on him, small as I am, with a weapon. I have a legitimate source of guilt, nonetheless, since I abandoned my mother to his cruelty, hoping that her invalid state would spare her from the worst of his rage. But our feeling of guilt goes beyond such rational considerations. We feel guilty simply for being outcasts. We are the undeserving, and our outcast state proves it. All our life we strive to show that we deserve better, Jean-Louis. All our life. Why do you think you come, in sheer kindness, to help an old man with his farm? Why do you save, at the risk of bodily harm, a man in danger of being crushed between a beast and a wall? Why did I, as you saw, fling myself between that beast and a child, and why do I labour every day to bring a little ease to the sufferings of our townspeople? Because we're good by nature? Perhaps. But certainly also because we're ashamed of what we are.

"Forgive me," he said. "I can sense that I am making you uncomfortable with my speeches. Why should *you* be uncomfortable or ashamed of what you are, just because I carry the burden of my own childhood in this form. I can think of no good reason. You are an active, resourceful spirit, that much I can see, and perhaps the Montmartre you carry inside is like a torch, and not a burden of any kind at all. They were certainly resourceful and energetic people, your adoptive family. Isn't it so?"

"Yes," I said.

"Yes, I think so. You know," he adds after a moment, in a different tone, "I am familiar with the Mon Chat Noir."

"You are?" I say, astonished, and momentarily a little anxious. *How* familiar? What else does he know?

"Oh yes. I should say, I *was* familiar. As you are surely aware, it has been closed for many years."

I nod, although it's the first I've heard of it.

"I don't say I ever knew the place well, only that I was familiar with it. I went there a few times, and to other places on Pigalle." He chuckles, a surprising sound on the water." I believe you are a little surprised, Jean-Louis, that I have ever left this *région*. Before I married Hélène, I travelled. I travelled outside France, also, when I was younger, to Italy, to North Africa even. And to Paris. The Mon Chat Noir was a delightful place. Its speciality, as you remember, were the English girls. I always liked the

English girls, I don't know why. Have you ever been to England, Jean-Louis?"

"No."

"Never? You've never been to London? Good heavens, man, you should go, while you're still young. There's good fun to be had, when you pull back that heavy covering of English coldness and reserve. The girls are not cold. I had the good fortune to be there on a visit during *la Guerre de quatorze,* when I was on secondment from the Ministry of War. At the beginning of the war, in '14 and '15, before the friendship went sour between our countries. While we were still friends, our ministry and theirs. And the girls treated us well, I can tell you that."

There was a streak of barely noticeable light, downstream, on the horizon, a smear of grey gradually acquiring colour.

If the thing had occurred to me, at that moment, that I realized later——dear God, how did I miss it? ——when thinking back on the old boy's words, I might have tipped him into the drink then and there, and held him under, just so as never to have to have that thought again.

But I was too sleepy, and too far gone in my involuntary fondness for the little piggy pile of a person beside me, to think, even for a moment, about his presence among the good-time girls of London in '14, and in '15, the year of my birth.

10. *Fathers*

OLIVIER DU GREFFAND IS OF COURSE NOT MY father, because although he was in London like a million other people in 1914 and 1915 when I was born, and spent time with good time girls like my mother just as countless thousands of people did, tens if not hundreds of thousands of people, there is no reason to think that he is my father given that, a) we don't look remotely like each other and, b) the odds are overwhelming against it in view of, as I say, the hundreds of thousands of other people who were there in London up to the same thing.

And, c) his eyebrows are not bushy. They're nothing like mine.

How evil is Uncle Reggie Peterson?

That's the only thing that continues to haunt me.

He's a very evil man, that's true of course because you have to be when you're plotting the downfall of Herr Evil himself, Adolf Hitler. You have to be prepared to sacrifice people. No-one knows anything about this for sure but it's rumoured that we parachuted dozens of expensively trained operatives into Holland and straight into Nazi hands when we knew, because we'd cracked the Germans' code, that their arrival place and time had been betrayed to them and that our agents would be captured as soon as they landed. But we sent the poor bastards nonetheless, Dutch men and women mostly, Uncle Reggie fully aware (and others? Churchill?) that they would all be captured, interrogated and quite possibly killed, just to make the Germans believe we hadn't cracked their code, the necessary horrid wartime logic being that although the Germans might believe we would sacrifice an agent or two in order to try and fool them, we'd never send 30 men and women to their death——damn it, we were English, and if there was any people on the face of the earth who believed that Englishness stood for moral probity, it was the Germans, the bloody idiots——just to help Hitler believe we weren't listening to his private phone calls.

The Germans did kill the men and women we dropped into Holland, after torturing them first. This was the rumour I heard. And I imagine they did it to make sure we paid dearly, just in case sending the Dutch agents was indeed a bluff or a feint or a tricky move in the game.

So if Reggie Peterson was evil enough to dispatch a whole planeload of agents just in order to bring off a *feint*, what compunction would he have in sending me off on a mission with a singular sting in the tail?

What I mean is, I'd always suspected that Uncle Reggie had found out who my father was.

And I knew he'd never own up if I asked him.

Then again, if Edie herself didn't know, as she insisted (and Harry Seltzer told me the same thing, "I'm sorry, Alan, old son, she honestly doesn't know and that's the truth"), how could Reggie know any better than she did?

I had a pal called Basil at Merchant Taylors, at any rate he was a pal until I confided a little too much about my secret life (my thieving life, I mean, as well as my missing parentage) to him, and he said something that I liked to reflect on, with regard to my mysterious paternity. Basil was a Classics scholar, and he said I should see myself as being like Achilles, with a mortal mother and a God for a father. Basil said this told us that Achilles didn't know who his father was. 'Son of Zeus' was apparently a designation by which, according to Basil, the Greeks meant "son of God-knows-whom."

I liked the idea of being Achilles, with Zeus or the like as a father.

It was a pity about Basil, but he was too toffee-nosed to have lasted as a close pal. I shouldn't have told him about my stealing, but he seemed to enjoy the idea of delinquency of an experimental nature (we'd discussed possible revenges we might take against various teachers and prefects we hated), so I thought I could trust him. He kept away from me after that. But at least he didn't shop me.

Perhaps you wouldn't shop Achilles, no matter what you knew he'd done.

11. *Solange*

I THINK I WAS GETTING A LITTLE complacent about the absence of Germans in the district, and aside from moments of dizzily wondering whether I'd parachuted into another era or whether the war had ended or the Germans had withdrawn from the region, I had begun to relax in a way that field operatives should never allow themselves to do.

I was on my suitcase radio, in the middle of a broadcast to London, when the ancient Labaronnerie front doorbell rang and scared me half to death. The thing made a tremendous noise; heaven knows how old the mechanism was, since it was actually a bell-*pull* of the kind you might expect to find outside Dracula's castle. But it was loud enough to raise the dead, or at least to reach the ears of a deaf old farmer in his distant kitchen.

Luckily I wasn't in the middle of a word, since it would have alarmed London if I'd shut down in mid-transmission. When the bell clanged, I'd re-broadcast my demand for confirmation of ODG's identity as the correct 'Anita' target, and received the same bland answer as before: *Clear to kill.* I'd have preferred the addition of some phrase along the lines of *id confirmed* to show that at least they'd registered my concern as something other than a bout of funk, and I was feeling slighted enough to make my dissatisfaction plain in a further reply. To do so was perilous, as I was well aware. No-one makes a transmission without a close eye on the clock, and if I tapped in another communication I would be keeping the line open for longer than I had on this or on either of my previous missions. The absence of a German presence in any form whatsoever, since I'd landed, may have been at the back of my mind, encouraging me to take the risk, when I prepared to send my new message. *Insist,* I was going to say, on a reconfirmation, but just before I began, the bell rang and I jumped out of my skin.

I'd heard no-one arrive. At a first glance out of the window, from behind the curtain, no-one was visible. It was the middle of the day, 12:17 precisely as I knew from the watch I had sitting beside the radio suitcase. Was it possible——the worst fear always comes to mind first——that they had the whole place surrounded? I moved swiftly back to the suitcase, closed it and stowed it in the little wardrobe opposite the foot of the bed, and went cautiously back to the window.

At the very moment I peeped out, I met the eye of a person looking up at my window. I'm sure that Gordon Molesey, our surveillance instructor, would have raged at me for my ineptitude, but what can you do? It never works like this in the movies, but in reality, unless you have a mirror you can hold at a conveniently surreptitious angle (nothing looks more suspicious from outside a window than someone's hand appearing, holding a mirror), you either do look out of a window or you don't, and at the instant when you look, you're likely to be visible.

Looking up at me, holding a bicycle on which she had come and on which she was evidently preparing to leave again, was a young woman with a square jaw and fashionable shoulder-length hair, dark and dense and seemingly as solid as a hood or hat of some kind. She didn't look like a member of the occupying forces or even their advance guard. As she raised a hand, to greet me, I thought, but then I saw that it was to shade her eyes as she inspected my window, I made myself visible and raised a hand in greeting.

HER NAME WAS Solange Bourget, and she wrote, she told me, for the *Courrier Paysan,* a local newspaper whose origins apparently went back to the French Revolution. She had heard about the incident on market day, as had many people beyond as well as in the town, indeed the whole *région,* if you believed Solange, and she had already interviewed *l'un des deux héros,* as she put it, one of the two heroes of the day. In the course of their interview, Dr du Greffant had kindly told her where she could find me; she hoped I didn't mind.

Solange seemed like one of those eager beavers who are too eager by half, too bright-eyed and bushy-tailed ever to strike anyone as having found their proper rut in life. Professionals in the making, like long distance runners, are noticeable by the minimum of effort they make in the early stages. But she loved writing for the *Courrier,* as she told me several times, and although I had no intention of letting her write about me, it was nice to spend some time with an attractive, enthusiastic person my age, for a change

She was also, I thought, somewhat taken with me, on sight. I know this will seem like a further piece of absurd vanity, as if Runt Rawlinson were Casanova in his own estimation. But what can I do? It's the truth. She even said, within five minutes of meeting me, that although like everyone in the town she knew *Oncl'* Albert, the old patriarch of Labaronnerie, she had never known he had a handsome cousin, and where had the Garçonniers been hiding me?

Well, she was a flirt. And that was fine with me. It was also her technique, I dare say, for getting interviews. She had brought a camera along, to get a snap for the paper of *héros* number two, and she probably thought that the word 'handsome'——*beau,* which in French always seems to me to have thrilling undertones of 'beautiful' in a way that 'handsome' specifically avoids——would encourage me to agree.

It didn't. If nothing else, and I was already a field operative contravening every rule in the book by starting an affair with my target's wife, I knew better than to get my mugshot in the local rag. But I let Solange think I might consider it, so that she would go on flattering me a little more.

Searching for *l'Oncle* Albert, whom I knew to be baling hay in the most southerly portion of the property, I led her north into the sloping pastureland where I had landed on the night of my arrival. Solange said she felt she should at least say hello to Albert; I promised to do so on her behalf if we didn't run into him, as of course we would not, in the direction where I was leading her

I didn't seriously contemplate a kiss or a cuddle, let alone more, at midday in the blazing fields with someone I'd met only moments before, but walking with her through the empty pasture was deliciously arousing. If it's hardly the case (and I wish it had been) that one glimpse of Runt Rawlinson was enough to make maidens weak at the knees, it's certainly true that Runt himself, while on a mission, was in a permanent state of heat. Other agents have told me the same thing. The surplus electricity in your spirit, all the tension and the adrenalin, doesn't know where to go, and it winds up going to your cock. It's like having fifty thousand people screaming your name as you line up the ball for a shot on goal——I say that because I once spoke to a professional footballer who maintained that a scoring opportunity before a big crowd gave him an erection

Stumped for a story to give Solange, a Jean-Louis Garçonnier story, that is, in order to pad out her interview with me (which I asked her to keep anonymous, since I was quite happy to be *l'autre héros*, hero no.2, so modest that he refused to be identified), I resorted to the same stuff I'd been giving ODG the night before, on the river. To wit, the real stuff, my own Montmartre childhood transposed into my nom-de-guerre's life.

It was wonderfully warm and bright that day, after the rains of the night before, and the thistles and the cow parsley had been roused to a last spurt, waving in the sunshine. The dandelions, the *pissenlits* so beloved of French cooks, made a golden carpet for us, and it was lovely to imagine that in a parallel existence where I really was Jean-Louis Garçonnier, I had come to help out a short-handed, elderly uncle and tripped over the love of my life, here in a little country town. And now we were idling through the *pissenlits,* both knowing already that we had found our destiny in each other. She even let me take her hand.

To amuse Solange, and to see her wonderful toothy smile again, I claimed that Gérard and I had sneaked in to see the immortal Mistinguett, thanks to a backstage pal at the Casino de Paris. It was a complete lie, but I couldn't help elaborating on it, and soon Gérard and I had found our way, in my story, to Mistinguett's dressing-room, reaching it before she did, hiding beneath the wonderful dresses hanging in her dressing-room closet, and trying not to giggle when Mistinguett entered, her performance over, with no less a visitor than the President of the Republic and his bodyguard. While the bodyguard stood outside the door, the President and the diva proceeded to give us, his amazed listeners, an object lesson in the French way of sex, complete with instructions, exclamations, orgiastic cries, and mutual congratulations.

I realized I had gone entirely too far when I saw Solange's grinning, delighted face. "This you have to let me tell for the newspaper," she cried, and pouted when I had to insist that I had only told her in the strictest confidence.

Below us, as we climbed out of the pasture and onto a rough track, a stream was visible, with an ivy-covered building beside it. Solange identified it as a watermill, now disused and replaced by a more powerful mill, with a petrol-fed engine, in a neighbouring valley. She knew all about its history, and as we walked down the track towards it she told me that the Garçonniers had milled their own grain there for their private use, since the 18th century, and fed their animals on it. The Garçonnier feed was said to have contained a special combination of minerals drawn by their oats and barley from soil rich in phosphorus, zinc and the like, which explained the once-famous yields of the Garçonnier herds. An envious town mayor, who was also a rival dairy farmer with a grudge against the Garçonniers, had retaliated by secretly diverting the stream——this was the rumour, Solange said, unproven but widely believed——that came down from the mountains and fed the watermill, gradually depriving the waterwheel of sufficient power to turn the millstones. A more scientific and less intriguing tradition held that climatic changes had simply enabled the river where Olivier and I had fished to accumulate the meltwater that had once ended up in the millrace. All it took was a millimetric shift in the water table, over the period of a century, to put a watermill out of business, the scientists had declared. But everyone still preferred the tale about devious Mayor Choumert and his vendetta against the Garçonniers. I watched Solange as she told me the ancient town gossip and sketched long gone local characters. This was her element, it seemed to me, and she reveled in it.

The ruined building still stood proud and tall beside the mill race, which was full of bright weed hiding the water from sight, and we were able to clamber up the old stairs and make our perilous way across the rotting timbers of the top floor, to look out across the sunny Garçonnier acres. Perhaps I could have stolen a kiss, as we sat on the windowless sill, happy to be alive and young on such a glorious afternoon, gazing out across France in all its summer array. I was quite proud of myself for basking in the moment as it was without gambling for more, at the risk of losing it all. I watched Solange's dense cap of hair swinging beside her face like a bird's wing, and imagined, as I studied her strong profile, the children she would have in years to come, for whom that profile would spell safety and merriment and all things motherly. She would retain that eagle nose and strong chin into grandmotherhood, I would have been prepared to bet. And if Providence permitted, perhaps I could one day return to the town and meet her children, if not her grandchildren. From all she told me that day, she knew the town, its corners and its characters, so well——as a budding journalist, she was its perfect chronicler, and her job only added to the bond——that I could not imagine her ever wishing to leave this place.

And if it hadn't been for the job to hand, the mission London was apparently still determined that I should complete, I'd have been able to dream that I too might come back here one day and find myself a corner, a cottage as old as the mill, perhaps, in one of the brilliant green fields below us, laced with gold and purple blossom.

12. *Love on the sly*

WHEN I TOLD HÉLÈNE WHAT HER DEAR husband had asked me while we were fishing, that as a favour to him I should visit her to provide enlightening and entertaining conversation, she simply nodded.

It was an uneasy nod, and I gathered from it that she wasn't surprised, and that she shared, perhaps, my sense that our feelings of guilt were easier to bear if our relationship was entirely sneaky than if our meetings were sanctioned. It was worse, somehow, to have been invited to associate by the very person who would be most hurt if he knew what we were really up to.

Or would he be? Hélène's unease certainly implied that he would, but her nod suggested that she knew already that a welcome had been extended to me to spend time with her in Olivier's absence, as often as I liked. So what else was agreed between Monsieur and Madame?

Finally, in a cynical moment as we were tidying the bedroom together——after what I think was our third encounter——I asked her whether the freedom of the apartment that her husband had offered me was supposed to include the bedroom. Her reaction shamed me. She stared at me for a moment with her end of the counterpane in her hands, then let it fall and sat down on the bed, facing away from me. When I reached her she was crying. I was as sure as ever I had been when I first met her, that she was no actress. I saw in her face not only the anguish caused by our affair but, quite separately, a measure of fondness and pity for Olivier that stabbed me, as well it might. When I made to comfort her, she pushed me away. At the door to the apartment she said it might be better if I didn't visit her any more.

I knew she was right, and for several days I stayed at Labaronnerie and did more press-ups and training drills than ever before. I transmitted to London the pointed query, Any messages? And received no answer. Somehow I managed to stop myself returning to the town, and until I heard Albert climbing the stairs and calling out to tell me of a phone call, *"C'est pour vous, monsieur——une femme quelconque..."*——*some woman or other, for you*——I had begun to think that it was over. But the *femme quelconque* was Hélène, her voice shaky, begging me to return.

THREE IN THE afternoon became our time. *Trois heures de l'après-midi.* Any weekday except Thursday, which was Fernande's day to clean the apartment. 3 p.m. was safe, any other workday. It was Olivier's busiest time at the office, Hélène maintained.

All the same, no such rendez-vous in the marital home is foolproof. I'm sure she knew it as well as I did. One day I was lying there in bed with her amid the awful du Greffand furnishings (heavy dark heirlooms, presumably hers by origin rather than his, 19th century chests and wardrobes *de province*), both of us puffing away on our post-coital Gauloises like two lovers in a French film, when we heard footsteps in the corridor.

C'est lui! Hélène cried in a melodramatic whisper. "It's him! He wasn't feeling himself this morning and I should have guessed he might——"

I hushed her with a hand over her luxurious mouth. "Listen!" I said.

We listened. The footsteps were clearly female by their click-clack.

"Fernande?" Hélène whispered. "But it's not her day."

"Then who?"

"She's the only one who has the key. She and Olivier."

"Does he ever wear high heels at home?"

She gave me a sour look. Humour, especially in a moment of peril, was not Hélène's strong suit.

My ladylove threw on a chiffon robe in which she looked, I thought, even more provoking than when she was naked, and peeped out of the bedroom door.

"Fernande? C'est toi?"

"Oui, Madame," came a rasping voice from the far end of the corridor.

"Mais qu'est ce que tu fais içi?" What are you doing here?

"Ne vous dérangez pas, Madame. Je nettoie dabord la salle de bain."

Listening to Fernande telling Hélène not to worry and that she would start with the bathroom, I had a queasy instinct that I was being set up. I looked round for an escape route, but on inspection the third floor window offered none. Now hearing the voices recede, I stepped to the bedroom door and peeped out into the apartment.

"Mais c'est Mercredi, Fernande," Hélène was saying, reminding her that it was Wednesday and not her usual day, Thursday," *c'est pas Jeudi."*

"Oui, Madame. Pourtant je vous ai déjà dit, la semaine dernière, que mon beau-fils vient demain de Paris."

As I listened to their receding voices, Fernande insisting that she'd warned Hélène of the arrival of a relative and that they'd agreed to the switch of dates, and Helène insisting that she'd done nothing of the sort, I slipped out into the corridor, still stark naked but clothes in hand.

To my alarm, the voices and the footsteps abruptly turned back and became loud enough for me to judge that they were almost upon me, with a calmly protesting Fernande in the lead.

I opened a door, stepped into what proved to be a closet, and closed the door, wasting an instant to congratulate myself on my quick thinking——Runt in his element——before starting to slip my pants on.

Or intending to slip my pants on. No sooner had I closed the door than it opened again to reveal Fernande, with an appalled and speechless Hélène behind her.

Trust the working classes in a tight spot, I thought, as Fernande reached past my naked body to seize a mop——I was in the broom cupboard——and a bucket.

"*Bonsoir, m'sieur,*" Fernande said with impeccable tact and without a moment's hesitation.

Ah, the French! you might think. And later I did wonder whether Fernande's sang-froid might have something to do with the presence of other *m'sieurs* in her employer's life and even in the marital apartment, over the years. I even wondered, despite Hélène's furious denials when I charged her with this, whether such rites as the one I endured were a part of Mme du Greffand's relationship with Fernande, a quid pro quo, even, for Fernande's silence.

"*Pas mal,*" I imagined Fernande remarking smoothly to Hélène the following Thursday, "*le p'tit bonhomme de Mercredi.*" Not too bad, your little Wednesday chappie.

I'D BE TELLING a lie if I gave the impression that the sex was somehow still the mystical cauldron of our first afternoons. Sheer surprise had been a part of that, and the way we were both caught unawares, I think, by a force of mutual desire that drew on positively occult sources. As for the inner bandages I broke through because Hélène was who and what she was, mother and mate at once——well, you can only burst out of your bandages one time. They'd taken nearly thirty years to accrete, and I wasn't planning to start the bandaging process again.

Nonetheless it was profound and always wrenching to revisit that first shocking breakthrough (I couldn't help wondering if she too had tapped into some reservoir as ready to spill over as mine had been), and in place of its savage excitement and the astonishment that had accompanied it, a tenderness began to grow which was uncomfortably like love. It was like friendship, too, and we both knew that was the safer, wiser port to steer for. The only port, really. When I was able to acknowledge fully the sheer unappealing sadness of her face in repose, I was also able to release the fondness it inspired, an emotion that had been no part of our first furious encounters.

I knew that sooner or later I would have to make use of our intimacy to further my mission, and at last I cooked up a stupid story about having been told by someone in a café, some stranger with whom I'd fallen into conversation, that Olivier had friends among the occupying forces.

Was it true? I asked. Was he in league with *les Boches?*

"To do what?"

"I don't know," I said.

Hélène seemed frankly and unforcedly surprised. Amused, even. We were lying in bed, flesh to flesh, in that wonderful time when two bodies seem to share a smell and even a flavour, as if our acidity and alkalinity had merged to make one perfectly compatible seedbed.

"Who said this? That he has 'friends'? You mean German friends? Who said so?"

"A man in the *Paradis Des Jeunes,*" I said, "in the market square."

"What man?"

"Just a man."

"What's his name?"

"I never learned his name. Big square-faced fellow, wide shoulders. The English *milord* type, with red cheeks," I said. I'd seen such fellows in the square, farmers who looked as if they'd come here from the shires, en route to one of the crusades, stopped off for a beer and never left.

"I don't know anyone like that. The man must be an idiot." She studied me. "Or trying to make trouble. Some dissatisfied patient of Olivier's perhaps, or one who wanted to be treated for free, like all the rest. "I nodded, but she was still gazing into my eyes. "You don't believe me?"

"Of course I believe you."

She said nothing.

"I was just curious," I said. "I mentioned Olivier and poum! out of nowhere, the man says he belongs to the *sympathisants.* German-lover, he said. *Ami des boches.*"

"People say that all the time, about lots of people."

I bided my time, caressing her hair, her forehead.

"When you say, 'who wanted to be treated for free, like all the rest,'" I said, "do you mean that *maquisards* expect to be treated for free?"

Now her gaze rested on me more searchingly.

"You're very quick, Jean-Louis, to understand that."

"And the Germans too, perhaps, expect to be treated for free."

"*Pas du tout,*" Hélène said. *Not at all.* "They always pay. The soldiers and the army officers are honourable men. I could tell you many stories of their decent behaviour.

Better than the French army would be in the same situation."

"So," I said, "Olivier tells you who pays and who demands free treatment?"

"Why wouldn't he?" She was studying me again. "And you're wrong if you think he treats the *maquisards* for free. He makes them pay. That's why your fellow in the square is putting out lies about him. Olivier's not so popular with the *maquis*."

"Then perhaps if France remains a province of Germany, he won't be sorry?"

"Why do you say that?"

I shrugged. "People talk about reprisals against the *sympathisants*, when the Germans are defeated."

"People talk about all kinds of things," she said. From the way she was looking at me, I wished I hadn't persisted down this avenue. "You say, when the Germans are defeated. Are you such a defeatist yourself? I thought you approved of Hitler's views."

"I'm only repeating what I hear, Hélène. And wondering how it must be, to be a prominent member of the town, like Olivier, and walk a line between the different forces. It can't be easy."

Hélène shook her head, upset now. "Is it so hard for you to understand him?" she said at last. "He doesn't care. People are people, they still get sick, without getting permission from the government or from anti-government."

She turned away, on the pillow and lay with her back to me and her body folded into mine, its fulcrum still hot and moist against my groin.

"To understand Olivier, you have to know about his father, who was a *gendarme*, very brutal. It makes Olivier sick to his stomach to see a uniform, or even a gun. When he explains that he's a pacifist and people get angry with him, he defends himself with ideas. But the truth of it has nothing to do with ideas. It's his father. The man who beat him, and his mother too." She was silent for a time. "Now you know."

OTWPYWPSTYTPPRPSDMCTADTKYPTERPOFPMFN
    Fear target error, I tapped in, adding onto the end of it my previous, repeated demand to double-check ODG's identity, and hoping to God that someone bright would be on the receiving end, bright enough to take my plea for further reconfirmation seriously.
    But the same damn message came back:
    egtwpybufgg
    The same words, for the third time now. *Clear to kill.*
    What now, for God's sake?
    There had been nothing new in Hélène's portrait of an innocent Olivier who looked at Germans and *maquisards* and said, A plague on both your houses. Olivier who was neutral, because of the *gendarme* father. Or for whatever reason.
    I knew all about the *gendarme* father.
    And none of it, not one piece of it, was conclusive.
    Cumulatively, though, it was starting to get to me——the tone of Hélène's voice, and Olivier's too. A tone with the dull ring of truth.
    There was only one way to find out for sure whether ODG was or wasn't involved in undercover political work (because if he wasn't, how on earth could he have betrayed and tortured Marie Marquand?), and that was to contact the local *maquis* directly. Then speaking as an SOE operative (with the DSO in the works——or maybe with the medal on the line, it occurred to me, and that was why I hadn't been informed yet: perhaps it was dependent on

this mission!), I'd ask them whether du Greffant was one of them or not, yes or no.

What I couldn't do was ask London to put me in touch with someone in the local Resistance *réseau*. They wouldn't send a name over the airwaves, I didn't think, no matter how confident they were in *When to the sessions of sweet silent thought*. Worse still, Reggie would be told that I was baulking. London would already be wondering what my problem was, given that I'd found the target ten days ago and had three Clear to kills and was still seeking reconfirmation. Reggie would be fretting. If I now radioed for directions to the nearest *réseau* he would reckon that I'd either lost my nerve and was playing for time, or that I'd lost faith in our planning machinery and was trying to play a solo, rather than a bolo, part, doing my own fieldwork and seeking to draw conclusions of my own. Field operatives don't do that. They do what they've been told to do, and bolo home.

But I don't need Reggie, it occurred to me. I've got Albert Garçonnier.

The old boy might not be an active *maquisard,* and to judge by his working hours on the farm, seven days a week, he wouldn't be high on my list if I was looking to recruit in the district. But he had a Resistance contact whom he trusted sufficently, and who trusted Albert sufficiently, to agree that Albert would put me up and sponsor me as his relative. It was a brave undertaking, on Albert's part. He was very possibly a dead man if I was caught and forced to reveal where I'd been staying——which in any case the du Greffands knew, along with others in the town, perhaps, whom they might have told. Or would Albert be able to maintain that I had simply shown up out of the blue, claiming to be a longlost relative and willing to work for food, at a moment when this was just what Albert needed?

The Germans would never buy it.

So far I had sought to involve Albert in no espionage chit-chat at all, so that he had the minimum of information to betray if we were rounded up. We'd carried on as if we really were uncle and young cousin. In fact, during the days of my exile from Hélène, when I knew I should be planning ODG's assassination but was moping around missing his wife's embrace instead, I tried to distract myself from my lover's woes by throwing myself into farmwork, and to Albert's amazement I cleaned out the entire cow-byre, forkload upon forkload of heavy, stinking deep litter. I strained a muscle in my back but I got it done, and disinterred the whole of the previous winter's bedding, before spraying the byre and scattering a fresh layer of straw.

Albert's expression, when he saw the result, had been well worth the labour, strained muscle included. He stared, then turned to me with something almost approaching a smile on his ancient face. His eyebrows lifted, as if to say, How d'you manage this, then?

"*Suis Garçonnier, moi*," I said. Chip off the old block.

Albert nodded, and then inclined his head towards the farmhouse. I followed, and a home-brewed bottle of beer was forthcoming from the cellar, sweating with cold.

NOW, WHEN I pinned the old boy down in the kitchen, the evening after my most recent inconclusive Morse-code talk with London, and told him I needed the name of a local *résistant*, preferably someone high up in the organization, old Albert stared at me in puzzlement across the table. The boss, if possible, I added.

Knowing he was a little deaf, I was about to ask him again, when he shook his head.

"*Mais tu la connais*," he said.

And for a moment, time stopped

You know her.

I knew her?

Oh wait.

Please God, not Hélène du Greffant.

That would be more than you could handle, said my heart.

It was like seeing that you'd sliced yourself with a knife and then waiting in that strange timeless instant, like seeing the ball struck on a distant tennis court and waiting for the sound to reach you, waiting for the news that yes, your eyes had told you true and pain would cruelly confirm it, any instant now.

Hélène? Hélène fooling me while I thought I was fooling her, Hélène who, to be fair, had no reason to tell me who and what she really was, since I had given her no reason to think me anyone or anything other than Jean-Louis Garçonnier, drifter, idle seducer visiting a country relative——*that* Hélène? Hélène who pretended to be pro-German but whose disguise of a Hitler-*sympathisant* (dear God, could she really be the very opposite, a resistance *chef de réseau?*) was exactly the one I'd adopted myself on entering du Greffant Towers...

Hélène who had all day to scheme and manage a *réseau,* Hélène who hid her true role from her husband no less than from me? Or——

Or the two of them together——

And myself the dunce, thinking I was duping them both?

Or had I actually fooled them into thinking I was an innocent passer-by?

All these thoughts whirling in a long moment as if seeing my life from the other side of a mirror, the charade of my life in which I thought I was the one watching and scheming and crafting my role, and which now stood revealed as someone else's creation entirely, a play in which scheming Runt was just another character——

And then Albert spoke, seeing my horrified bafflement.

"*La p'tite Solange,*", he explained, adding "You met her last week, you told me."

Wait. *Little Solange?*

Solange, eager flirtatious Solange with her bat-wing hair and her motherly profile? My Solange?

Whom Olivier du Greffand had told where to find me——this was my first thought when I regained my balance and Hélène had retreated, in my mind to the loneliness of her books and her boudoir. Solange whom ODG had sent to me, at Labaronnerie.

Solange who, then, had really only been here to interview me for the *Courrier Paysan*? Or who had guessed something more?

Solange, of all people.

"Do you have her phone number?" I asked Albert.

He nodded, still studying me, presumably trying to make sense of my evident stupefaction. Wasn't I myself allied to the *maquis*? These English, he might have been thinking, they certainly know how to keep a secret. Even from themselves.

13. *The millrace*

IT WAS A DULL DAY, THAT FRIDAY. TWO weeks exactly since my arrival out of the sky.

Two weeks. Two tumultuous weeks, when you put all the events together. But most of it consisted of waiting, and the waiting made it seem a whole lot longer than it was.

There was time enough to establish little rhythms of familiarity, knowing when Albert was working which part of the farm, knowing the du Greffands' timetable in town. I hadn't seen Hélène since Wednesday, because Thursday was Fernande's day to clean. I wasn't entirely sorry to take a break from ODG Towers. Quite possibly Hélène wasn't either. My suspicions about Olivier must have started to strike her as more than idle curiosity.

In every way, it was time to settle 'Anita' and leave.

I retraced my steps that morning, on the way to the old watermill, following the path Solange and I had taken, the previous week. It seemed unfamiliar now, and several times I took off on a tangent before deciding that I'd been on the right path all along, and turning round to walk back to the place I'd branched off. The dull weather made the pasture itself seem surly, barely recognizable as the fields of joy of our earlier excursion. The fields of Scripture was the phrase that had entered my mind, walking through them with Solange. Now it seemed an absurd connection to make, fuelled more by incipient romance than piety. They were just fields, and no doubt I was losing my way because at the time I'd been paying less attention to them— —Scripture, indeed!——than to Solange herself.

Our phone call had been brief. Remembering how frustrated Solange had been when I wouldn't let her write my Montmartre memoirs in her *Courrier* column, I took my cue from this and asked her if she was still interested in my tales of Mon Chat Noir for her newspaper. *My tales of my black cat.* As I said the words they sounded so much like SOE code I almost laughed. Solange, too, I thought, would be using coded communications often enough to be struck by the same thing.

She said she was of course extremely interested in my story, and I asked her to meet me at the mill, at the same time as last week.

As she agreed, and hung up, I went through a normal SOE procedure that this, the first call I'd made during this mission, brought almost automatically to mind. I stayed on the line, listening, and heard a tiny sound that might have been no more than a minute interruption of the signal, a mere blip on the line. Or it might have been someone else hanging up. Rural French lines, as I knew only too well, were subject to frequent interruptions, crossed lines, and loss of connection. An eavesdropper's paradise. I had no reason to think it was old Albert listening in, since I'd seen him go out to his regular ploughing duties, and had waited for him to leave. Besides, as far as I knew there was no second telephone in the house.

It was time to be done with it all. As I went through my routine on Friday morning, I pictured Hélène waiting, reading, trying to read but unable to concentrate, watching the clock until she could begin her own preparatory routine of bathing and powdering and perfuming. And finally applying make-up. Hours of preparation for a few minutes of pillaging. But no doubt building up the mask was as much fun as tearing it down. I pictured ODG in the office, patiently listening to familiar woes. I pictured Solange beside her bicycle, testing the chain, adjusting the mudguards, setting out.

Which of these images was a sham, was wrong?

AT LAST I knew I was on the right path, when I emerged at the bottom of the pasture full of *pissenlits* and thistles, and saw ahead of me the little track that led down to the mill that nestled in the valley, as if on a grassy knee. Below it the land fell away again, into a gorge too wide for the meagre stream that ran through it now. You could see by the size of the channel what a torrent had once come through, no doubt for millennia. Now the water trickled down to the mill from the hillsides to the west and north, and barely disturbed the millrace with its speckled weave of water weed. Even from a distance, the race twinkled with its miniscule blossoms, like a knitted shawl full of tiny bright knots that someone had made for it and thrown across the elongated rectangle of water.

A part of the old water wheel was visible too, I realized as I approached. Its warped and rotting paddles had a sinister air, like something rescued from the depths, some part of a gigantic paddle steamer or the screw that drove a giant submarine.

I couldn't see Solange. Perhaps I was early, or she'd been detained——please God not by the police.

I climbed up to the window at the summit, on the top floor of the mill, where we'd sat and gazed out, the week before. The timbers creaked and sighed. One or two bent perilously underfoot, sending me back to find a safer route. The top floor was darker today with just the pale, seedy light filtering in through broken tiles, and I made my way by feel as much as by sight towards the single window in the south-facing gable end.

Settling on the windowsill, I tried to trace by eye the route Solange might take if she were coming from the town, across the fields. After a time, tension took its habitual toll on me, and I fell asleep. This tendency, which was the very opposite of relaxation and which I understood to be my body's refusal to tolerate sustained stress, had got me a reputation as the supreme *shag* artist. To be able to sleep under pressure seemed to others to be the ultimate in *shag*. I was *shag* man personified. I was happy to give this impression, but in reality I would have traded it for sustained alertness. Unless there was someone beside me to nudge me awake when showtime arrived, I was capable of sleeping through it entirely.

For a moment I thought it was dark when I awoke, but it was only the heavily clouded sky masking the waning afternoon light. A chill wind was blowing, clattering the loose boards and shutters on the draughty building.

"Solange?"

I called her name a few times but got no answer.

Then I saw her bicycle parked neatly on its stand, tucked into undergrowth, mostly overgrown laurel, at the back door. Had it been there when I arrived?

"Solange?"

I went back into the building and called again, and I must have walked around the whole property, up and down the mill race, calling, wondering if she, in turn, was searching for me, or had gone for a walk while waiting. No matter how late I was I would know when I saw her bicycle that she was still in the vicinity and would be back.

I must have walked past her half a dozen times before I saw her.

There was no reason to look in the water, until at last there was a reason because time had gone by, too much time, and there was a reason, although I didn't want to name it in my mind, to look everywhere.

What I had thought to be the faintly uneven surface of the sweet bright quilt of weed on the surface of the millrace wasn't simply uneven. There were tiny breaks where the weave had broken and re-formed. There were several slightly raised, slightly humped shapes making a geography, a landscape in the otherwise flattish weed. Finally I realized that what I was staring at, in the weed, under a faintly rounded protuberance and between the stretched green knit of weed wasn't dark water but black hair, a thick black mat of hair dark as a raven's wing.

14. *Fin de partie*

I HAD A FRIEND WHO WORKED FOR THE River Police. Recently, this is, after the war. He always said the best of it was seeing the city from the river. If it hadn't been London's main thoroughfare, over the centuries, then it certainly had to have been its swiftest. You were at the Embankment and ten minutes later you were at the Isle of Dogs. That was the best part of the job. The worst was the floaters, especially if they'd been in the drink long enough for the fish and the crabs to have got at them and eaten away most of the face. That was fifty years ago when the Thames still had fish and crabs and such. But he said the other thing about floaters was that they didn't seem to want to come in. You'd get the boathook tucked into their clothes, hooked round a collar or a belt, or you thought you had, and as you pulled them in they slipped away. They wouldn't come. It was as if they belonged to the water now, and wanted nothing of dry land, not even a grave.

I wanted to pull Solange out of the millrace, even though when I turned her over in the water I could see the kiss of life was out of the question. There was a dull gash on her head that might have happened by falling against the concrete of the ten-foot wide basin that formed the race, but I could see no stain anywhere on the concrete rim. It seemed unlikely anyhow. A blow to the head had stunned if not killed her, and the water had done the rest. It would take a remarkably cynical coroner to come to the conclusion that this was an accidental death. But that was exactly the coroner's verdict in the matter of Solange's death, as I discovered many years later.

If I pulled her out and lay her by the millrace, on the cobbles————

I wanted to so much, out of respect, though I don't know why I felt this would show respect. Simply to leave her there floating in the water felt sickeningly callous. But if the police were to mount a serious investigation (I wasn't so trusting as to assume that they would do so, but I didn't want to prejudice the possibility that there was one honest policeman still at work in the region), then they needed to see the crime scene as it was.

I let her roll back until she was face down once more, and watched through tears as the green shroud of the bobbing, parted duckweed slowly began to reunite over her body. It was coming together over her a tender sheet, I wanted to feel; but all I could think of was the capillary cancer that Edie said had crept out of Aunt Sara's womb and coated her organs.

WHEN I GOT back to Labaronnerie I assembled what I thought I would need for the evening ahead and went down through the empty house and out via the kitchen, noting details as I went, because it was supposed to be part of our job and I hadn't been doing enough of it in the last two weeks.

I borrowed the raincoat and the bicycle again, and cycled into town. The clouds kept promising to deliver their cargo, getting lower and lower and rolling across the sky in long cylindrical shapes like the fingers of a teasing god, but the rain wouldn't come. At the *Paradis des Jeunes* in the square——only the French, in their florid manner, could name a greasy spoon *The Young People's Paradise*——I used a phone that had no second click on the line after the phone call ended, and informed the police, anonymously, about Solange and where they could find her.

Then I had a *pastis*, my first sip of hard liquor, and only my third drink of alcohol, after the du Greffands' suppertime wine and Albert's bottle of cold beer from the basement, since arriving in France. It wasn't technically forbidden (try stopping spies from drinking), but it was hardly advisable when you had work to do. On the other hand it was a cold, nasty day with colder and nastier deeds ahead.

I reached du Greffant Towers at 4:30 on the dot. The rainclouds were low enough to stroke the rooftops, and my sad blackened little tree, poking out from under the neighbouring roof, was wreathed in wisps of fog. It looked like a tree in hell, and the whole street now stood revealed, I thought, as its gloomy self,, not an expression of the joy of cities as a coming together of men but an expression of the costive, venal French soul, pinched and mean and murderous. It was a hard, barren little street, built to crush green life and keep it under. More than that, it was the world we had made, not just the French but all of us together, so that we could connive and kill and blow up buildings and build more. Living out at Labaronnerie I'd lost sight of reality just as I'd lost sight of the war. But now the town had spread its weather to the fields and brought death with it, and this colourless place was its epicentre, this little dank bare street with its cobblestones like cemetery markers huddled together in the gathering dark. Streets full of graves. Apartment houses full of sad women, each to their apartment and one on top of another, waiting for the killers to come home for the weekend.

I wasn't the only one who'd been drinking. Clearly by four o'clock Hélène had decided I wasn't coming and had decided to greet the stormclouds and the empty apartment with a bottle of wine.

She was beyond reproaches by the time, I arrived.

Mais, mon chou, il est trop tard, tu sais.

Her slurred words at the door informed me that we didn't have enough time to do anything before Olivier returned, or to do it and make everything seem right again. I didn't tell her it was too late for that.

There's always next week, I told her, knowing there wouldn't be. I wasn't very well disposed towards the human race at that moment, and had never lied more easily. I saw her face relax. I smiled and gave her a hug. I couldn't get the image of Solange Bourget's dead, sorrowful face out of my mind, with its redness around the eyes as though she'd been weeping, in death.

By now they'd found her, God willing, and lifted her out of the millrace and picked the duckweed carefully from her clothes and face.

I want a word with Olivier, I said, and told Hélène that in view of her husband's standing invitation to come and brighten her life with conversation, I was happy for him to find me here when he returned.

It's Friday, sometimes he's a little late, she said.

That's all right, I said.

If there are still patients waiting to be seen, sometimes he stays on a little.

I'm in no hurry.

We moved to the sitting room. On the way, glancing into the little kitchen, I saw the empty bottle and the glass she had quickly put beside the sink on her way to the front door.

And now, once I start the memory clock ticking, it's all there waiting inside me and I play both parts. There aren't two people, myself and Helene, or myself and

Olivier, just myself speaking for both of us in turn, as the memory unravels.

Un p'tit verre? A glass of wine?

No. Not for me.

Hélène settles and then realizes, embarrassed, that she's sat down on her book.

Let me see, I say when she's extracted it.

It's an illustrated book, a child's book, I think at first. *Les Aventures du Baron de Munchhausen.* I confess that I don't know it. One of her favourites, Hélène says, and I start to look at the illustrations of extraordinary feats and unlikely journeys.

Tell me something, I begin. Was Olivier at work all day?

Why do you ask?

I thought I saw him.

Oh yes?

Is that possible, Hélène?

You thought you saw him.

Yes, on the road to Labaronnerie. I was working with Albert, close to the road, and I thought I saw him go by on his bicycle.

(Now I pause and say:)

But perhaps it wasn't him.

It might have been him, Hélène answers. I spoke to him at two o'clock, to see how his day was going.

Oh yes? I watch the slow flush spread across her face. Clearly she phoned him while waiting for our 'three o'clock,' to make sure he was busy and had plenty of patients to detain him.

He was out of the town in the morning, Hélène says, visiting a dying patient.

I see. Perhaps it was him then, on the road.

She nods. *Peut-être.* Perhaps.

I look down and pretend to be studying her book, her collection of fantastic tales. He has a nerve, this ODG, to cover murder with a reference to a dying patient.

I was hoping, I say at last, that Olivier might not be too tired to accompany me on a little fishing trip. Tomorrow is Saturday, after all. No patients to see.

She gazes at me. I add:

The weather is bad, I know. But not for fishermen. I'm learning all about it from your husband.

He loves to fish, Hélène says. He'll probably go with you, even on a day like this. But are you sure you want to go fishing? You've been working in the fields with Albert, all day.

It's the perfect relaxation. Perhaps you'd like to join us?

She gives a short sad laugh of disbelief. From the way she's studying me I know I haven't succeeded in keeping an aura of finality out of my face and my voice. All the same, I oblige her to tell me about the unlikely adventures of Baron de Munchhausen with as much spirit as she can muster, until the sound comes of Olivier's key turning in the front door.

PERHAPS EVERY EXECUTIONER and his victim should be allowed a last journey together on a dark, silent river, waveless as Lethe, so that they can merge at last into Charon and his passenger slipping quietly away into the darkness, on the shoreless waters of death. Did he know it was coming? He chose to sit in the bow, with his back to me, unlike our first trip. Was this because he knew it was coming, and he accepted his fate? I wonder, at the time. Or because it was the last thing he expected?

As if the river is determined to mock me with memories of Solange, I can hardly cast my line without snagging in something, a floating clump of weed or a branch dragged down in the flood off the mountain. In the pitch dark, no moon, it's as if all around me lies another millrace, immense, thick with vegetation. Masses of weed heavy as corpses drift past out of the mist and bump into our little boat. Fish, too, come to my bait. Suddenly I can't stop catching fish. None of them want du Greffand's offerings. Your lucky night, he says, amused, as I reel in another. Your turn, tonight.

Does he really not know it's his turn?

I ask him whether his route to visit the dying patient took him out in our direction, past Labaronnerie.

Yes, north, he says. I went past Labaronnerie, if that's what you're wondering. I passed the house. Twice. Going and coming back. I thought of calling in on you, but I knew I already had a line of patients that would overflow my waiting room.

You didn't stop off, all the same, to pay a visit to the old mill?

Which old mill?

The old Garçonnier mill.

I didn't know there was one. Why would I stop off there?

The air itself, heavy and full of electricity, weighs on the water as heavily as it does on us. So Olivier has been telling me. It's the reason for the fish that come so readily——for me, at any rate——to the hook. A matter of air pressure, according to Olivier. In weather like this the fish go a little crazy.

Once, when du Greffand's cast goes awry, a rare event, and lands in my lap, I see when I detach the hook from my jacket, with the bait still on it, that he's using meager bait, a little articulated silvery grub made of plastic, which jinks like a tiny watersnake when it's reeled in, but isn't nearly as appealing to the fish as my hopping and dancing jitterbug lure. I realized he has deliberately reduced his own chances of a good haul, so as to give me a good evening's fishing and make up for my poor start the previous week. I say nothing. I'm hardly going to let him off the hook because thanks to him I've hit the jackpot with the crazy fish.

Have you ever killed anyone, doctor?

The circles we're floating in are as slow and gentle as the last time. But it's a lot darker without the moon. All we have is the little opaque light from the hurricane lamp, the glass discoloured and darkened by use. The lamp is wedged amidships in a metal bracket attached beside the gunwale and designed for the purpose. Its faint glow shows ODG's back, barely three feet in front of me. Our fishing baskets, full of bait and tackle, lie between us. In mine, under the tackle, lies the Welrod also. Du Greffand's head is sunk into his collar, concentrating as he flicks his line and reels it in again.

No, he says at last. You?

No.

We fish in silence.

You haven't helped a sick person to let go, say, before their time?

Perhaps. Helped? Yes. But it's not the same thing.

I dare say not.

It's time, and I'm ready, but some perverse desire to prolong the moment takes hold of me. I'm not trying to delay, because out there on the water in a tiny pool of dim light we could be in outer space, and outside time altogether. There's no hurry, hence no delay, I tell myself. I'm ready to do it, and unafraid. I only have to think of Solange, a stronger and clearer image now than Marie Marquand. But to be an executioner, in a moment such as this, it seems to me now, is to be a confessor too. If you ambush somebody and take them down before they can react, if you take a sniper's view through a telescopic sight, that's entirely different. This is like sitting with someone you've poisoned; they think they're still alive, but you know they're dead.

And now you're responsible for their last thoughts. For the way they will their life to eternity.

I hear myself asking him again about his childhood. Were there no happy times? Surely there were some happy memories.

Of course, ODG concedes. With Christian. Fishing and telling stories, as I told you. Skipping school, which made my father crazy.

He sighs, and I know he is back to the bad times once more. I persist, but now he doesn't want to talk, which is a problem, because some things have to be spoken.

Well, then, how about the good old days in Paris and London, Olivier? I suggest to him. I want to hear the lubricious old man once more, to stiffen my resolve.

Hein, Olivier? I'd like to hear about the good old days in London. Tell me more about the girls there. What were they like? Perhaps you could describe one or two of them. Can you remember any of their names?

Their names? I doubt it.

I bet you can remember one or two, Olivier, if you try. Was there a Maudie or a Flossie or a Margaret? A Trudy? A Sara? Give me some examples.

I really don't recall.

How about an Edie? Do you remember Edie?

No.

Yes, you remember Edie.

Why would I remember this Edie?

But you do remember her?

No.

Try. Try and remember Edie for me. What colour was her hair? Was she small or tall?

But he won't play, and a horrid silence now descends. Very well then, No more detours. I am not his confessor.

Olivier, you know why I asked you about killing someone.

No.

I'm talking about Solange. Surely you know that.

Solange?

Solange Bourget. The girl you sent to me.

I know Solange. How did I send her to you?

For the newspaper. That was the story. You gave her my address, so that she could write about both of us, and our adventure in the market square.

I told her you were staying at Labaronnerie?

You don't remember?

ODG says nothing. Perhaps, he says at last.

Of course you remember.

If I let slip where you were staying, Jean-Louis, he says at last, it was because——

Let's not play games, please. You knew she was *maquis*.

Précisément. That's why I mentioned where you were. Because of the interest you said you had.

That's why you sent her to me? So, in that case, why didn't she try to recruit me?

I don't understand.

She never mentioned resistance work. That's what I'm telling you.

If she didn't, I don't know why, Jean-Louis. She was probably waiting for you to take the initiative.

But you'd told her of my interest.

No.

You just said so. You said you sent her to me because of it.

Yes. That was why I told her where you lived. I didn't tell her about resistance work. It was up to the two of you. I am not a matchmaker for the *maquis*.

Why not, since you are in the *maquis*?

Now ODG sighs and shakes his head. If that's your idea, he says, I hope you have been telling the right people. I mean the people who would look after *my* interests one day, if de Gaulle comes and takes the country back.

That's not how it would be, Olivier, and you know it, if the Germans were defeated and you survived. You killed Marie Marquand. You tortured her and let her be taken away to her death. Did you think this would never come to light?

There is no room in the boat, to turn, without falling in. You can only paddle to shore, and then the first man, the man in the bow, gets out, and if there is a second man he follows the first one into the bow and onto the shore. But there's no turning round, on the water.

At last his voice comes. Jean-Louis, I don't know where you get such ideas. I've never heard of this person. I've never tortured anyone. Except my patients.

He has the nerve, or the sheer bravado to put some humour into his voice.

Some of them will tell you I torture them because I don't medicate them enough. But even that isn't my fault. I don't have enough medication. No-one does.

And Solange Bourget, Olivier. You killed her too. When one of your stooges at the telephone exchange listened, yesterday, and heard us make the rendez-vous, and informed you, you came out this morning and killed her at the watermill.

Solange? You're telling me Solange is dead?

As dangerous as it is to move, he now tries to turn around to me, but I turn his head back with the barrel of the Welrod.

You're an excellent liar, Olivier, I say, pressing the gun needlessly to his temple. After all, who was there to hear us, and what could they do if they did?

But I no longer believe you.

I pull the trigger, feeling the recoil as the gun and ODG's head jump away from each other. Then everything slows down into Runt-time. I even have time to pull the trigger again, aiming at the back of his head and thinking, one more for the Runt. For Edie. But nothing happens when I pull the trigger. Of course: damned Welrod, it's a single shot gun. One chance and one only. But it's all right. The impact of the bullet has pushed him to the left and he topples quite softly, with less noise than a flailing fish, into the river.

WHEN I REACHED the shore I took out the hurricane lamp along with my basket of tackle, and pushed the little boat back out into the river. For a few instants I saw it slowly start to spin, and then gradually vanish into the foggy dark. I took the Welrod out of my basket and hurled it after the boat, hearing the splash. And once I'd located my bicycle and identified the way back to the road, I abandoned the hurricane lamp as well. It might have come in useful later, but there was no point in taking the risk of drawing attention to myself if I didn't have to. There was no knowing who might be watching.

Earlier that evening I had kept a close eye on ODG in the time between his return home and our setting out for the river to fish, to be as sure as I could be that he didn't make a phone call during that time.

Hélène, of course, if she was in on the game, could have made a phone call as soon as we left, and alerted whoever it might be. Whichever side. Both, perhaps.

If she was suspicious of me. I couldn't be sure, and so I made my return to Labaronnerie as quiet and circuitous as possible, approaching it not from the road from the fields to the north of the house.

It was as well that I did——in all probability I wouldn't be telling this story if I'd approached the house from the front. Parking the bicycle by the side of the barn where Albert would find it in due course, I moved silently around the farmhouse, keeping an eye on the windows. Eventually I took up a position to one side of the drive, in a large stand of rhododendron, and waited, smoking a cigarette 'skilfully,' as we used to say, hiding the glow of the tip at all times.

Someone must have opened the door that led from my bedroom to the corridor, because the little flare of light that this threw into my darkened room was enough to show the silhouette of a man who was already present in the room, close to the window, waiting in darkness. Pisspoor tradecraft, I thought. By his peaked cap, he was a German. I hoped Albert wasn't already lying in the basement, beaten senseless.

Not much I could do, with my spent, single-shot Welrod at the bottom of the river.

Nothing, to stay for, then. The radio and my other things the Krauts were welcome to. It's not as if they haven't seen a suitcase radio before, even Type 2. They've got enough captured ones to set up their own *réseau* with them.

I thought about going back to the barns and taking the bicycle, but I was in no hurry at all now. I didn't need it.

I know it might read like sour grapes now, but I didn't particularly want to radio my triumph back to London. I didn't feel in the least triumphant; and I didn't want to be whisked back to Britain by Lysander either. I wasn't remotely ready for debriefing, and at that instant I had no desire to see Uncle Reggie's ugly mug ever again.

I didn't even really want to go home, although I didn't have anywhere else to go. I'd do my bolo under my own steam. From my first mission, I knew a man in Perpignan, a Spaniard by origin, Artemisio Valdez. He walked people into and across the Pyrenees, for a fee. I had the money, having spent almost nothing in the course of 'Anita.' And there was nothing I wanted to do more than walk, quietly, through the night (which was Artemisio's style).

I stubbed out my cigarette in the soft, deep tilth in the shelter of the rhododendron leaves, moved carefully through the undergrowth until I emerged onto the turf that lined the drive, slipped through the ironwork fence, and set off across the dark, fragrant pasture.

First I'd walk to Perpignan, which might take me ten days, and I'd do it Artemisio's way, at night, when if you were on a road you could see a car coming half a mile off and hide. And sleep during the day. If I could sleep. But it wasn't sleep as such that I felt I needed. What I wanted was time to try and leach the previous two weeks out of my soul.

15. *Runt, DSO*

I NEVER DID LEACH OUT 'ANITA', ON THE way home, or later, for that matter. But at least I got back in one piece, and not too shaky, all things considered. I was still alive to the disgust I'd felt, when I thought about it. But under control.

I took my time. Spent every sou of my Anita-money, in Spanish bars, and on Spanish girls.

I didn't care if London thought I was lost or dead or that I'd made a run for the border and was hiding (which was more or less the case). They did think I'd been captured, when another week passed and they hadn't heard from me.

If they'd had the resources, Uncle Reggie claimed later, they'd've sent somebody in, someone who was already in the region and could go and sniff around, to see what the story was. But we were gearing up for D-Day, and no-one cared much what was happening in the South-West of the country. The aim at that point was to disrupt the movement of the *Das Reich* tanks as they funneled north towards the battle zones. It was every agent to the pump. Some historians seem to believe that SOE played a decisive part in the Normandy Landings and the overcoming of the German attempts to repulse the invasion, by holding up the Panzer tanks, which arrived a month late largely thanks to the combined guerrilla tactics of the *maquis* and our own field operatives. Could well be. We certainly did our best.

"Why didn't you take a *train* to Perpignan?" they said at my debriefing.

Because I quite fancied getting out alive. Because I'd been blown. Remember?

"Not necessarily," they said. "You didn't *know* that."

No, well, when you're on a mission in France and you come home to find a German in your bedroom, the chances are he's not your new bunkmate.

"They still didn't know what you looked like."

Of course they bloody did. They'd have tortured it out of Uncle Albert, first thing.

"Perhaps Albert wouldn't have given them your description. Perhaps he'd have given them a false one."

Perhaps he said I was an African with orange hair. Why don't *you* go out there and ride around occupied Europe on your rail-Perhaps card?

Pillocks. *Still bolshy as ever* was probably what they wrote under 'Conclusions.'

The reason they wanted to know why I hadn't gone by rail, or got Artemisio to find someone with a radio so I could call a plane out to Perpignan to collect me, was envy, pure and simple. They kept plugging away at this because by disappearing into the hills I'd managed to get myself a few days' holiday in Sunny Spain while they, my debriefing panel, were stewing in a wet British summer. It was more than a week, in fact, that I spent in Madrid, in a total stupor, but they didn't have to know that, and in order to fudge the missing time I made my trek to Perpignan even longer, in terms of days supposedly spent on it, than it really was. Fuck 'em.

Each night, on the way to Perpignan, the first few hours of walking had been a kind of bliss. Smells carried each change of scene in darkness, each new field, each new crop. The sonic echoes of my footsteps measured distances to right and left, like radar. My tread, advancing as steadily as a mechanical device, sewed up the waiting flaps of verge. They fell into line and came together at my feet. With every step I turned the night into a seamless garment behind me.

Strange how that became my unconscious meditation, on my trek: working on aunt Sara's chiffon skirts, passing them carefully under the needle, as I worked the treadle. *You're such a good little seamstress, Alan. You'll always be in demand when you grow up.* A part of me had always yearned to go on working with cloth and thread, but knew only too well that if I showed any interest in it, at public school——let alone at military college——it would have undone all my hard work becoming Runt the Renegade. But in my mind, and in my hands I still felt the smoothing caress as the material submitted to its shaping. Now I was walking a hem, stitching France together clip by clop.

Every night began that way. Alert, not quite on auto-pilot yet. Cars sometimes passed, onrushing light like a tidal wave flashing over me as I flattened myself, full length in the grassy, unweeded gutter. Then hup-two-three, Captain Runt. Back on my feet and on my way. King of the darkness.

And then as deeper silences fell, as the moon rose or the mists descended, the voices came and once more I was hearing Solange's chronicles and Hélène's cries, and ODG's tales told to the river, his words bouncing back to me from the shore as I sat behind his humped back. There was a bear in the bow, waiting to be shot. Waiting to topple slowly sideways while I pulled the futile unresisting trigger, over and over like a killer in a nightmare, and no matter how hard desperately I pulled, no further shots came. Would he topple? Would he go, at last? Or would he turn, to grab and take me with him? The instants moved so slowly it was hard to know whether time was still working at all.

I got my DSO. They couldn't very well deny it to me, regardless of my bolshy-Runt act. I'd done my bolo. Killed my man. If every mission had gone as well as 'Anita,' we'd have been——well, we'd have been exactly where we were, in the war. But MI6 would have peeved as shit with nothing to point to in the way of blemishes on our record.

So I got my medal. True to Reggie's expectations, I haven't laid eyes on it since '44. In fact I'd lost the stupid piece of tin within six months. Things have always turned up trumps for me, though. People thought I was the last word in *shag* for turning up on parade without my red-and-blue on my breast.

Truthfully, I don't know if they really gave me the medal for killing my man. (Did they suspect something, even then?) I think they gave me the DSO just for showing up again like a bad penny, after they'd unofficially declared me lost. Plenty of others never showed up in the camps or anywhere else. They got dumped in a shallow grave somewhere, or slung into a quarry. Or a river.

I suppose it was Hélène I was worrying about, most of the time, when I got home. What if they'd never found him? We weren't more than 20 miles from the sea, and if Olivier's body was washed all the way out, I don't suppose he'd have floated around forever. I imagine that even corpses finally get waterlogged, or their clothes and boots do, anyway, and sink. So he might never have been located and identified.

Of course if Hélène had known all along what he was up to, or that despite all her guff about his neutrality she knew he'd been up to *something*, she wouldn't have been all that surprised if one day he didn't come home. But if she really hadn't known——and he'd just disappeared——

Or else, if he turned up dead, on the riverline or the seashore, or spotted by a fishing vessel or caught in their nets, dead with a bullet in his head, then the last memory she had was of him going of fishing with Jean-Louis, her lover. Who'd vanished at the same time. If Hélène had known nothing, it was quite a legacy I'd left her. Would she have beaten the bushes to find out who her husband had really been?

I couldn't get Solange Bourget out of my my mind either. Solange, in her duckweed shroud, surfaced in my dreams. Why in God's name had I thought I'd make an assassin?

Self-torment was pointless——you had to know when not to take responsibility for the entire war. (That was Uncle Reggie's phrase, not mine. Clearly he could see through my jaunty disguise, which I dare say was the same as everybody else's.) It was poor Marie Marquand, tortured before she was killed, whom I ought to keep in mind. Whom, one way or another, I had avenged. That had been my job, and I'd done my job. I said that to myself over and over until I pretty much believed it. So did everyone else. I was the avenger, I'd stuck it to the bastard who betrayed Marie. PM says well done, Reggie muttered to me one day out of the side of his mouth. Churchill knew who I was!——knew what I'd done for England and for him!

SOE would never forget me (at least until everyone forgot SOE).

Neither did they send me back to France, though. Too valuable, they said; too important as a resource. Needed, to instruct others. Why go and risk spoiling a perfect record? Just for a bar to your DSO? Stick around and teach and have people look up to you. Let 'em touch the hem of your robe.

I always thought it was really a punishment for taking the lazy, lovely route home from France. Walking through the Pyrenees, taking buses across Spain—— everyone else had to wait till the war was over.

"The bugger even got back with a *tan*." That was what they said.

Underneath the tanned, shag exterior the good old Runt was falling slowly to pieces. Drinking too much; that would have been a clear sign to anyone who cared about me, but I hadn't let anyone come close enough for that, not for years. Not ever, really. It's a tribute to how completely at odds I was with myself that the closer peacetime came the more I dreaded it. What would I do out of uniform? (I who'd always believed I was the very antithesis of a uniform.) How would I manage in world where my DSO didn't precede me into every room, but would be luggage not required on the voyage, at least until my obituary? (I who'd taken trouble to lose the damn thing.) What would I actually *do*, in a peacetime world?

I CAN'T IMAGINE what I was thinking——I wasn't thinking, is the only possible answer, just acting in a spasm of fear——but when the Germans finally surrendered I got myself seconded to military intelligence at GHQ in Hamburg, with the rank of Major. Everyone else was stripping off their wartime kit like kids racing to be first into the water, and what was I doing? Re-enlisting. Nobody wanted to be in Hamburg, or at least no-one that I met there. I said I spoke German, which was a complete lie, in order to get the posting, and no-one challenged me on it. In fairness, half the people in Intelligence there couldn't speak the lingo either. They'd signed up for the same reason I had. They dreaded being de-mobbed and returning to their lives or wives or both, and they fancied some free schnapps on the last Easy Street they were ever likely to know.

Major Rawlinson, DSO, formerly of SOE's F section, had it pretty good. Whispers (*hero!*) followed me around. Nobody expected me to lift a finger, except to interrogate a few rogue Brits who'd got so deeply into the black market that they were giving our own occupying forces a black eye. This was pretty hard to do since the locals knew we were all on the take from the beginning and they didn't expect anything else. I had the honour of interviewing a few of these rogues (my sort, every last one of them) alongside the honourable Kim Philby, later famous as a Communist spy and defector to Moscow, but at the time my fellow-interrogator and a super-rogue if ever there was one. When I knew him he was a pretty convivial fellow, and even fonder of schnapps than the dishonourable Runt. If you didn't like schnapps you could get any kind of liquor under the sun in Hamburg's Free Port, or free-for-all port, as we called it. Never mind liquor, the saying was that you could buy anything there from a racehorse to a Rembrandt, or for that matter from an antique astrolabe to an atomic scientist. Some people made small fortunes. I was too shag for that. I was working on my breakdown, getting drunk and molesting the Fräuleins.

There were a good few breakdowns, after the war, among SOE survivors. Some people had taken the strain of missions and packed it away about their person, partly because wartime London wasn't the ideal place to let off stream, and more because we were told to hold our water, in Reggie's stupid phrase. One day when the show was over, the mouldy little package of accumulated terror blew up, slicing through a person's nervous system like shrapnel.

Some people can't manage a decent breakdown, though, because they're built like a submarine, in sections with steel walls between them. Lose one part, seal it off, move into the next. That was me. Eventually you're just so full of liquid that instead of sinking or blowing up you just keel over onto your side, like a dead body toppling off a small boat on a river in France, and lie there mouldering and waterlogged.

It never ceased to worry me, consciously I mean, the business of what exactly had happened to Olivier's body. Of course, that would be one quick way to go mad, wouldn't it? Worrying about the disposition of everyone you might have killed in war.

EVENTUALLY EVEN OUR military occupation of Germany came to an end, like all good things. There was only one thing I dreaded more than the prospect of trying to find a corner in civilian life, and that was the company of my fellow officers. I'd had a good long run. Time to quit.

Shamefully enough I became one of those ex-soldiers I'd always derided, who held onto their rank in peacetime like a drowning man clutching a spar. *Major* Rawlinson, if you please. DSO. Moustache, cafeteria and bar. Nowadays, if I spot someone who knew me in my postwar guise, I'll slip out of the room, if I can, or cross the street before a cry of "Major!" pins the tail to the poor donkey I was then.

I even held the damn rank before my face when I crawled back to Harry Seltzer to ask him for a job managing one of his furniture outlets. *Major Alan Rawlinson*, it said on the wooden desk shingle, announcing who I was. *Major Alan Rawlinson, Regional Deputy Manager.* "We're proud as punch of you, Alan," Harry said. Proud to have your name on the shingle, in all its glory.

He hadn't seen much of me for eight years. Neither had Edie. But they'd probably heard stories. It's hard to be a secret lush for long. They must have just been hoping that all it needed was a quiet spell on civvy street, time to recover from the shocks and alarums of war, and I'd settle down and become a steady little runt, Regional Deputy Manager and before long, who knows, Regional Overlord, Gauleiter and Reichsleiter himself.

I lasted three months, and that was only because Harry bailed me out half a dozen times, calling me in sick and even standing in for me, on occasion, before everyone knew what my problem was. At that point I could have been Heinrich bloody Himmler and I wouldn't have got any respect. Major *Trawh*nson they called me to my face, after one salesman at the Hendon branch where I was working brought in a story that I'd been seen pawing girls in Soho, so drunk I could hardly stand.

I wept and begged Harry, played Major Crawling-son and promised to reform, but Harry knew my fame would follow me round the stores——*oh it's the famous stepson, is it, how are you, Major?*——so most of the jobs he helped me get in the next few years were in other fields where he could call in a favour.

Mostly office work. I was useful (when sober) to have on an interviewing committee. *And this is Major Rawlinson, DSO.* Before us sits the candidate, aged 22; seems to have barely begun shaving; is too young to have fought, and looks passably impressed. *Pleased to meet you, Major.* Even when not entirely sober: just sit there, shut up and look gimlet-eyed. John Mills in a moustache.

I worked in stationery, or rather oversaw the sales reps for a stationery firm in Old Street. I worked, until fired for turning up drunk, for an American company recruiting keen young British salesmen with a posh accent.

Worked as a sales rep myself, for an old distinguished firm of haberdashers. Farjeon and Nephew. (All I wanted to do was take a course in dressmaking, but how could I even tell them this when all I was trading on was my pinstripe suit, my weathered face and little moustache and valiant war record? How could I tell them I'd personally sewed a zip into the road to Perpignan, one hundred and fifty miles of it, at night, with not a slipped stitch or a broken nail?)

I'll be honest with you, those years are a bit of a blur. I suspect they were a bit of a blur at the time. I can remember waking up in places I'd rather never have been, night or day. You don't need a description.

THE HORROR OF 'Anita' only opened up for me at last because like a fool I couldn't leave it alone.

Neither did I try and directly pursue the old traces, after the war, and go back to France to disentangle what had really happened or find out what had ensued, as a good many operatives did. Morbid buggers, most of them, I thought. Christians looking for absolution. Or just poor ordinary haunted soldiers, I suppose.

I'm having none of that, I said loudly and firmly. (Of course I bloody wasn't. Did I want to go back and run into Hélène? Some chance.)

But I couldn't let it entirely alone, either.

Books came out. Rumours went round. Documents were declassified. I'd have done better to steer clear of my old SOE pals, as I did later on, but at the time I was still telling myself I was proud of what I'd done and proud of my medal (wherever the darned thing was). The more that other people, genuinely shag people, started to turn their backs on wartime derring-do the less ready I felt to have done with it myself. Wouldn't it always be my moment in the sun, my moment of glory? I could cultivate being shag for the rest of my life, I could be as shag as you liked and no-one would ever see anything impressive in it again.

I was reading the section about post-war reprisals in France in *Heroes and Heroines of F Section* (yes, you can find me in it, not exactly a chapter to myself but my name and a decent summary of our work in the Tarn-et-Garonne, with the word 'fearlessly' attached to our assault on Tansonnier bridge, and probably cleared by Reggie Peterson in advance——you'll understand what I mean if you read the book, which is cautious and mealy-mouthed in the extreme) when I came across a name that troubled me. Reggie himself had warned me that the assassination of Olivier du Greffand, along with Churchill's role in approving it, was still an official secret, so I shouldn't expect to read about it in the public prints. But here amid a list of names I couldn't help noticing someone called Claude Geffant, said to be a wartime collaborator who had disguised her collaboration——*her* collaboration, since this Claude was female——beneath resistance activity. In other words, a double agent, whose death in the months after the Armistice was among many that were judged by the authors to be "most likely not an accident."

Geffant, not du Greffand. Hardly identical. And not a man. Not even a doctor, as I discovered when I probed a little deeper, recruiting old SOE pals to help me delve. Not a doctor at all; according to what I could find, she had been a dog-breeder. But——and this was the detail that got my attention——she had lived in a village not fifty kilometers from the town where my mission had been set, and where Marie Marquand had disappeared into the claws, I had been told, of Dr Olivier du Greffand. Geffant; du Greffand. It nagged at me.

If this Geffant had worked with Marie, and some third party had known the name only by sound——suppose, now—and when the information had been double-checked by someone imperfectly acquainted with *maquis* activity in the area but familiar enough with the town to know the name of one of its leading doctors: what then?

It was a leap, a stretch. But it was nothing compared to some of our cock-ups, whereby a foreign name repeatedly mis-typed might end up unrecognizably distorted.

All I had was Geffant, Mademoiselle Claude, breeder of poodles (did this sound like a double agent?), possible collaborator, dead in '45 in a suspicious multiple crash involving a *remorque*, a trailer truck. To get any further than this I would have to go back in person.

But go back and risk coming face to face with Hélène? Over and over I told myself I didn't have to. The facts were circumstantial, regarding du Greffand's guilt. But so what? They were bound to be, short of a confession. Wasn't that sufficient?

I sought out Teapot Armstrong, that solid old survivor now running a company he started himself, managing security for large office buildings; Teapot on whose account my 'Anita' dossier and its description of Olivier du Greffand had been based. He said he'd told London everything he could recall about Marie Marquand's betrayal from what he'd learned at Buchenwald——an account which was already third-hand when it reached him.

Du Greffand or possibly du Geffand, or Geffant? Teapot could only shrug.

He could see the anguish in my eyes, as much as I tried to disguise it. I knew he wanted to say, Let it go, Runt, we all have to let it go sooner or later. But he could probably tell I wasn't ready.

And he certainly wasn't offering me an executive position with his security firm.

He was patient with me, though. To amuse me he brewed up a cup of tea in the famous, tiny, battered little teapot that had given him his nickname, the one-cup metal pot he'd carried everywhere with him, on parachute drops into France and even in and out of concentration camp. "I'm trying to remember, Runt," he said, watching me sip my tea. He'd reported the information passed on to him about Marie Marquand as best he could recall it at the time, he said, when he got back to London. And SOE had presumably checked it out and then written it up. Yes, Marie had been tortured in a basement by her betrayer, that's what he'd been told. Du Greffand or du Geffant——that he couldn't swear. Or Geffand. Man or woman? Teapot recalled it, he said, as a man. But what if the information was already wobbly, he added, when he received it himself?

"Look," he said at last, "have another cup, and I'll tell you a story."

Once the water was brewing, Teapot began.

"Chap I knew. In Buchenwald. I've never forgotten this, Runt, and I swear I try and live by it every day. Jewish chappie. But he was in with us lot, with the politicals. At the risk of giving away the point of my story, that's really the gist of it. He was in concentration camp as a political prisoner, and he was executed, while I was there, as a political prisoner. He was actually a Jew, but the SS didn't know that. See, he'd done everything in his power, when the Nuremberg Laws were passed and he could see that as a Jew he was dead meat, to enable himself to pass as a gentile. He changed his name. He changed his appearance. He had himself made all kinds of elaborate fake documents showing that his parents were the Baron von this and the Baroness von that. And he even paid some real, impoverished, childless German nobility to swear, if it ever came to it, that he was their kid. And when I say changed his appearance, Runt, you won't believe what he fucking went and did. He not only had a nose job, he had a fucking foreskin sewn back onto his dick. I'm not kidding you. I saw it——he showed it to me because I wouldn't believe him, that he'd had it done——and it was fucking horrible. It looked like what you'd think. It looked like someone had sewed a foreskin back into his dick. But there it was, and possibly it might have fooled a half-blind person who wasn't looking very hard.

"Anyway it never came to that, because one day in the street our man saw some Jews being arrested and beaten and he couldn't stop himself from watching it happen, and a Gestapo bloke behind him, someone our man couldn't even see, says Heil Hitler and before he can think our man forgets his expensive new name and the nose job and the fake foreskin and instead of obediently repeating "Heil Hitler" he says aloud, "My arse," *Mein Arsch*, not meaning to, not even knowing he's spoken aloud. And the next thing, he's arrested too, not for being a Jew but for disrespecting the Fuhrer. "My arse." That's all it took. Two syllables, and he's in Buchenwald. So I always think of him, poor old My-arse as I call him, who wasn't there in our barracks one day. He wasn't there because they'd taken him to the execution block, I don't know why. Perhaps it was alphabetical, and the fancy German name poor old My-arse had taken was probably von Arsehole or something beginning with A. That'd be just his luck."

I was sipping my tea as Teapot concluded heavily for me. "You see what I'm telling you? What will be will be. Just as I was meant to escape from Buchenwald, that poor bugger was meant to end his life there, exactly as he feared he would. All the fake names and nose jobs and sewn-on foreskins in the world couldn't change that. He just said, My arse, like you'd breathe out, without thinking, and what gave him away was who he was, which you can't get a doctor to alter surgically for you, not at any price. What happened on 'Anita,' to you and to the other people caught up in it, was going to happen to you all anyway, in some form or other. That's what I'm telling you. That's why you have to let it go. Not because it's all right that you might have killed the wrong bloke and caused unnecessary death and suffering. It's not all right at all. But because what's written is written. You can't duck out of it. So you may as well just say to yourself, could I, Runt Rawlinson, have changed the workings of the universe? And quietly answer, My arse. Okay?"

16. *The journey home*

THE NEW MAYOR WAS A SMALL NEAT
man about my height, with the face of a handsome rodent,
and a charm which seemed wasted on town politics in
South-West France and really deserved, it seemed to me, a
wider stage. I almost wanted to ask him, Do you sing? And
point him towards the career his face and manner
suggested. But he was a genuinely nice man, perhaps too
nice for a glamorous but cutthroat existence in showbiz.
And perhaps he knew this. He'd had quite enough
excitement, he told me, as an aviator for the Free French.
He neither wanted to be airborne again, nor even to visit
Paris again. His childhood sweetheart had waited faithfully
for him here in the town, they now had three children, and
he was deeply grateful for a well-rooted and serene life.

I was amazed to be talking to him at all. Amazed to be
standing in the *Mairie,* an ancient, airy, completely
refurbished house overlooking the market square. Below
us——I could see it all the time, out of the window, and
couldn't help staring at it——was the rectangle of paved
stones where I had saved Olivier du Greffand from the
bull. How I longed to tell the story to this charming,
civilised man in his tie and blue blazer! He seemed so
much to represent the present and the future, and even the
very setting-aside of the past, that he surely wouldn't arrest
me if I identified myself as a player in those long-gone
events, events which featured both courage and cruelty
and murder in a darkness and confusion long since
dispelled. But I knew I mustn't succumb to the sunlight

streaming in at the huge windows and the airiness of the room and the people circulating in the market square below. It was only an illusion that wartime was a world before the flood. Of course the good mayor would have to investigate, in the name of France and of the Free French. In any case, I didn't dare risk it. I'd got this far, into the man's office and his confidence, as an author, supposedly, working on a book about the region. It would not do to reveal myself as the con man I was.

I never really thought I'd hear back in the first place. Despite Teapot's sage, calm advice, I had to go; Teapot wasn't living with my duckweed nightmares. At first I assumed I'd simply have to go back to the town and brazen it out, pretend to be a visitor, hope no-one recognised me and that I didn't run into Hélène——(yet wasn't that the whole point, to run into Hélène? To find out what happened?)——until I came across someone who could tell me how things had turned out. I'd written blindly to the *Mairie*, saying I hoped to write a book about some of the heroic work of the *maquis* in the area, and would there perhaps be a local historian prepared to meet and talk with me? It was astonishing to receive a brief polite letter from Lucien Berry, *Maire,* the mayor, inviting me to make myself known to him if I was able to visit the town.

I found myself a hotel—a small hotel, although in a town that size there were no others, and in the slow recovery from war I was surprised to find that there was one at all——and hid, too scared to go out. On the phone, I spoke to an employee at the Hotel de Ville and made an appointment to see the mayor in the morning. Looking in the hotel bathroom mirror, it had belatedly occurred to me that now, if ever, was the time to use the disguise skills taught to us by Colin Burke, our actor-instructor during the SOE years. The smallest changes, Colin always said, are the most powerful. Not false beards. Just a change of hairstyle. Thicker eyebrows. ("Or in your case, Runt, thinner," he'd said, to general laughter.) That's all it took to make you unrecognisable.

And who did I think was going to recognise me anyway, after eight years? A red-faced English-*milord* famer-type who'd glimpsed me once in the *Paradis des Jeunes*? The barman there, perhaps, when I'd only been in there three times at most? Old Albert Garçonnier, if he'd survived his treatment at the hands of the Germans the night of my escape (indeed if he'd survived whatever subsequent treatment they handed out)? That's if he was still alive, even supposing he'd escaped Nazi clutches and gone on farming after the war. He'd been deaf and ancient enough eight years ago. So surely not old Albert. No-one, then, apart from Hélène. She was the one person in the whole town that I was hiding from. Hardly worth changing hairstyle and eyebrows for.

And I wasn't even hiding from her. It was the town I was hiding from, not the town as a place full of eyes and full of danger, but as the place that brought back memories of myself. It was some unexamined and unexpiated part myself that was out there in the town, that was waiting for me, wandering the town unshriven, and I couldn't leave the hotel for fear of meeting him.

IN THE MORNING I felt less spooked, and was able to look around and notice changes in the town as I walked to the market square, colour that had been absent under the hellish blanket of war. Even if much of the colour was advertisements on walls still old and peeled and grey, it brought hope. My old self was gone, like the old colourless town. It wasn't waiting for me; it had been papered over with ads for Charrier water and *Fanfan La Tulipe*.

I told Berry, the mayor, that I was a journalist and a historian. I'd planned to tell him that I'd been in SOE, and cite my experiences in the Landes and the Tarn-et-Garonne, rather than locally, to bear this out; but I was afraid this might put it into Berry's mind that I could have also been active in his region, so I left SOE out of it altogether. While researching a book on the resistance efforts in the South-West, and their aftermath, I said, I'd been led to write to him by a mention of a woman called Claude Geffant, hitherto unknown to me, apparently a resistance fighter. Yet she was the victim of reprisals after the war. Presumably, I suggested, she had been suspected of being a double agent.

Berry nodded, and sat me down; I opened my notebook, and we awaited a coffee. The shocks, however, were already on the way.

"Yes. 'Presumably,' monsieur," he said, sizing me up with what seemed like a kindly but penetrating eye, the eye of a wise rat. "Presumably is correct. For my part, I know only what I've been told. During these years I was in a Free French uniform. And I can tell some things about this period, for your book, not because I knew all the people personally, but from second-hand. Also I can speak, because most of the players are dead. Especially the man who was called *Oncle* Albert, who died three years ago. No-one could touch him because nothing could be proved, and he was an old man so no-one wanted to take their personal revenge on him."

Oncle Albert? Old Albert——my Albert?

We'd barely begun and I was lost.

"Revenge?" I said. "For what?"

"It's believed he was in business with both sides, the Germans and the *maquis*. A lot of bad things happened. I imagine you may have heard of a British agent called Marie Marquand. Rather she was not British or even French, she was Polish but she was trained by the British. And although Albert Garçonnier, which was his name, *l'oncle* Albert, was supposed to be her mentor in the Resistance, it's believed that he gave her to the Germans, because she was captured and sent to the camps. Where she died."

I must have been staring at him, I'm sure, because he repeated, "So, you have heard of her, I think. And before she was sent to the camps, they did bad things to her."

The coffee arrived, and Berry raised his cup in formal welcome. I could barely bring myself to do the same, in case my trembling hand betrayed me.

In the basement. In Albert Garçonnier's basement, where my cold beer came from.

In the basement, as described in my 'Anita' dossier. Where Marie had been tortured. Olivier du Greffand had owned no basement, and I'd shrugged it off as an error in my dossier without noticing that where I was living, my own 'mentor,' as Berry termed him, had an ample basement

"Albert Garçonnier?" I asked, pretending to study the notes I was taking. "That's the name?" Albert who I had last imagined, as I slipped away through the rhododendrons, captured, beaten, perhaps dead in his basement, at German hands. When in fact——

"An interesting story for your book," said Berry. "Albert Garçonnier was an old man with a grudge. Really it was his grandfather's grudge, not his. They say that one of my predecessors diverted the water from his land so that he had to abandon his mill. It was done out of jealousy, this how the story goes, and that Choumert, the mayor of the time, was a dairy farmer who wanted to get the better of the Garçonniers. But the sons, the Garçonnier sons, never forgave the town, and *l'oncle* Albert was raised to carry on the vendetta. Any way he could bring misfortune on the town, he would do it. You see how things happen around here? National politics has nothing to do with it. France, Germany, these are abstractions. Maybe a few bureaucrats or soldiers passing through, but then they leave again and the town is still here. It's about personalities, family history, feuds that go back four generations. What did *l'oncle* Albert care about Nazis or the resistance? He would put the fox in the henhouse. He wanted to see them all fight against each other and mutilate each other. And that old mill, the old mill that he had to abandon when Choumert diverted the water, was what started it all. During the war there was even a murder right there, at the old Garçonnier mill, where a girl who was the leader of a local resistance *réseau* was found dead. It's believed that she knew something that got her killed. Probably she knew that Albert was involved in the capture of Marie Marquand, or at least Albert suspected that she knew, and that she was ready to give him away to a paid killer from the British secret service. But *l'oncle* Albert got to her first."

I knew I had to say something, to prevent my face from giving me away. Put it away, I told myself, put it away, the image of Solange. "To a paid killer from the British secret service," I said.

"That's what they say."

"And Albert killed her?"

"This is all hearsay, you understand. Perhaps she just fell into the stream and drowned. Some people are foolish enough to climb a ruined building and hang out of the window. Who knows? There was never a verdict of murder in her death. You see, there's one thing you would always have to tell people, in your book, and that is that war is always a very confusing time. To give you an example, you asked earlier about Claude Geffant. Geffant was a courier for *l'oncl'* Albert, and probably the contact person for the British agent, Mademoiselle Marquand. Well, a person of a similar name to Claude Geffant, a Docteur du Greffand, was found dead around this time, shot through the head and dumped in the river. We think there was perhaps a confusion of his name, because he was not involved with the resistance or with collaborators."

Berry gazed at me from under his fine brows, his small dark handsome rodent face intent.

"Around this time also, a man disappeared who had been staying with *l'oncle* Albert at Labaronnerie, the Garçonnier farmhouse. He was perhaps involved in the whole affair, but because of Albert Garçonnier's different allegiances, who knows for which side he was working, this man? We know almost nothing about him, except from people who think they saw him in the town. He was small, like me. And like you," Berry grinned. "But with more hair than either of us, perhaps. Time diminishes us all."

"You think he was the paid killer?"

"Who knows if there was a paid killer? Other people say he was simply a young Garçonnier who came to help out with the farming when *l'oncle* Albert was all alone."

"What do you believe?"

"*Pardon?*"

"What's your personal opinion? Was there a killer? What do you think?"

Berry finished his coffee in a gulp, then gave me his quick dark rodent-glance again.

"I think I look forward to reading your book," he said.

I SAT IN the Paradis des Jeunes, trying to take it in.

Or rather trying not to take it in. If Berry was right, I'd been completely bamboozled by Albert Garçonnier, as had the SOE contact man who set me up as Albert's guest for the period of 'Anita.' Albert, not Olivier du Greffand, was the double agent. My host, if I'd only known, was Anita's real target, the man who betrayed and tortured Marie, and killed Solange.

As soon as I saw 'Claude Geffant,' in *Heroes and Heroines of F Section*, that otherwise dull and timid book, I knew it. I'd killed the wrong man, as I'd feared I was being told to do at the time, until Solange's death enabled me to persuade myself otherwise.

The little click on the telephone line. It had been Albert, who'd doubled back into the farmhouse. Later, when I retraced my steps on that fateful day I found it clear in memory that Albert's tractor was still under the eaves of the lean-to beside the barn, where it was always parked, and if this is a true memory it should have alerted me at the time. I had seen Albert leave the house and had convinced myself that he was already at work ploughing the fields before I made my phone call. And no doubt there was another instrument in the basement, where he'd been listening in, as I made the rendez-vous with Solange. Solange, who would have pointed me away from Olivier du Greffand. And towards the person who had been Marie Marquand's 'contact'; towards Claude Geffant. Who knew all about Albert Garçonnier.

To say it had been under my nose all the time was putting it mildly. How was it possible that I had ever thought I was an adequate undercover agent?

That evening I found at my hotel a note from Lucien Berry, the mayor, which I still have. It reads:

Cher monsieur,

Today you said of Claude Geffant that you believe she was killed in a suspicious car crash. Yes, but it was not suspicious because someone may have caused it, but more because we can't be sure that Mademoiselle Geffant was actually in the car. There were some possessions of hers, but the fire in the car made it impossible to identify the driver with any certainty. And since I have told you so many secrets already that I should say you will publish them at your peril, and certainly please without quoting me, I will tell you that there have been some rumours and several reports of people who claim to have seen Mlle Geffant in Indo-China, where there are many government agents. Supposedly she is one of these, she or someone who looks very like her, under a different name. Some of these people have a talent for survival, you know. In fact, that is their main talent, I should say. It's a talent of which we all need a little, n'est-ce-pas?

Avec mes sentiments les plus distingués...

Berry's signature follows.

IN THE PARADIS des Jeunes I did my damndest not to take it in but to review the whole thing administratively. I knew that if I sat there thinking about Olivier's last words as I put the gun to his head, if I now conjured up again the doctor sitting in the bow of his boat with his head sunk into his *veste*, talking about how the only torture of which he was guilty was of being unable to medicate his patients as fully as he wished——if I went there in my head I might be capable of going down to the river to see if I had the balls to drown myself, but I certainly wouldn't be able to face visiting Hélène du Greffand.

Which surely I now didn't have to do. Now more than ever. Surely I didn't have to do it. It would be the very last thing she wanted. So why on earth would I do it for my own sake, out of some contorted vanity of atonement, too late and almost certainly unwanted?

Administratively, then. Back to the nest of vipers I'd just uncovered. Think administratively, I told myself. No need to be surprised that I'd killed the wrong man, given the incompetence as well as the confusion that was now emerging as F Section's legacy. (And courage too, acts of immense, hopeless courage, yes, yes of course, but how many of them were a complete bollocksed-up waste of time and noble humanity?) *Clear to kill,* they'd said over and over, to a field operative who was havering and wavering, they thought. Or barely bothered to think, because at the time we were beginning to be administratively overloaded, and the skills that people like Uncle Reggie and Netta, mole rats disguised as gilded otters, brought to SOE in the early years, weren't so well suited to running a growing army whose coded traffic stretched resources to the limit. Errors happen in war, countless errors, and this time I'd happened to be the instrument.

Such generalisations had kept me going for years. What had finally damaged my belief in SOE was the discovery that SOE could have got Marie Marquand out before she was betrayed. As you may know, this was revealed to the public in the *F section* book, amid great breast-beating. A rare example, the authors wrote, or something to this effect, of the tragic costs of the game of war. We left Marie in the field and in mortal danger, in order to keep the Germans unaware that we had cracked their code, or at least in the hope of keeping them unaware of it, or to be brutally exact to contribute to the side of the ledger that would suggest to the Germans that we might be unaware that they had broken *our* codes. And yes, this *was* the game, and we all knew it. All through the war we lived with the sense that we were expendable, but individual cases were always explained away as misfortunes of war rather than deliberate sacrifices. But now, when I read in Lucien Berry's handwritten note that Claude Geffant might not have died in postwar reprisals but had been spirited out of France to continue her life as an agent abroad, I suspected (and still believe) that the game in question was even nastier than the authors of *Heroes and Heroines of F Section* knew. No-one would own up to it now, but in all likelihood Claude was one of MI6's longstanding moles. Marie Marquand was sacrificed as a pawn in this game, not even a pawn in SOE's war against the Nazis but a pawn in SOE's bitter rivalry with MI6, who loathed our fly-by-night, seat-of-the-pants style which trampled all over their carefully cultivated intelligence flowerbeds. SOE knew, I strongly suspect, that Claude Geffant was not a double agent who had worked for us and then, when she was captured, had been turned by the Germans and sent back to spy on us. She was in fact a triple agent, being run by MI6 under our noses (and the German noses) all the time, as she had from the beginning, reporting back to allow 'C', as MI6's wartime incarnation was known, to tell her what to reveal, and when, and to whom.

As SOE 'amateurs,', our hatred for 'C' was as ingrained in all of us as MI6 agents' loathing was for us. But it didn't justify sacrificing Marie and then making us mourn her as a heroine betrayed by the vile Geffant.

Or du Greffand.

And now I saw one further layer.

Was that Geffant/du Greffand slip not a clerical error at all? Not one of the Chinese-Whispers consequences of mishearing and mistyping, or sheer misinformation? What if it had been deftly planted by Mlle Geffant, using the happy coincidence of a similar name on her very doorstep, to point us at the wrong person?

Thanks, Claude. If that was you.

And now, when I got back to London, should I have chased that particular wraith to its lair, if it has a lair? Should I have gone back, found Uncle Reggie and confronted him, Uncle Reggie who probably knew nothing about the confusion of names or how it happened? Or should have I asked him to let me speak to some old SIS warrior who would speak, off the record, for MI6; who even if they were prepared to speak to me would tell me in the hushed atmosphere of his club that this was one of the many agonizing moves in the chess world of espionage, and perhaps even bribe me with a bar to my DSO if I would shut my gob? No, they wouldn't bother with a bribe, even though it would cost them nothing. Soon enough no-one would care who was killed or how or why, in a forgotten theatre of war.

The only thing to do was to repeat Teapot Armfield's personal 'mantra'. Could I have altered the workings of the universe? My arse.

Teapot, the only person to whom I imparted what I'd learned from Lucien Berry, told me many years later that Claude Geffant had finally died, this time in a plane crash close to the Laotian border. I said I didn't believe a word of it. Even triple agents have to die sometime, but I went on seeing Claude's hand in Indo-China. And if not Claude herself, because such people have ceased to have identities, let alone names, then a line of disappearing agents, slipping from town to town and country to country, leaving behind havoc, unexplained corpses, and boobies like me with a spent pistol in their hand.

Leaving poodles and lapdogs. A nice, humourous cover.

I had believed in my training, my dossier, my 'Anita' briefings and my handlers, without question. But that didn't let me off the hook. Not even 'My arse!' would let me off the hook. Wouldn't a halfway intelligent human being, let alone a trained agent, have been a little more skeptical? Good God, I was supposed to be——in my own estimation, at any rate——the runt, the renegade, the kid from the streets. Where had the Gérard in me gone, where had Alain gone, when I most needed him?

I COULDN'T STAY all day at the *Paradis*. I paid and left and tried to walk in circles to avoid going where I was going. One surprising addition to the town was a miniscule art gallery, where I stared at a mass of tiny paintings until I saw at last that they were rather beautiful. Oddly in proportion to the small room that contained them, these were miniature landscapes, bursts of light and colour, as if Turner or some such painter had dashed off richly coloured preliminary sketches on a telephone pad. Skies, mostly, here and there what might have been a tree, a hayrick or a house. Multiple shades of blue, or gold. The artist was a woman; I recall only her first name, Josiane. I wanted to own one, but felt I had no right to anything as beautiful as this, or perhaps more particularly to any piece of light and colour that rejoiced so freely in this landscape.

I wandered, but wasn't really wandering. I knew the way, and the town was too small to mistake where I was heading. A moment's uncertainty, seeing that the little stunted tree no longer poked its head out from beneath the roof, two doors down from the du Greffands. Then I was there.

I rang the bell, outside, in the street, waited with my heart pounding and the greater part of me praying she wouldn't be there. A crackle, then, and her voice, brusque, unchanged.

"Oui?"

I could still leave. I could still run, so that she wouldn't get to the window in time to look. I could still make it to the corner in time if I ran.

"*Je peux?*" was all I managed, *may I come in?* Without an introduction.

Silence followed, and then, after I was sure she'd gone away, leaving me to decide whether to press the bell again, or take my cue and leave, the sound of the buzzer came and I pushed at the heavy door, and went in. The stairwell and the winding stairs were like as pregnant with smell and sound as if I was back at school. I climbed the spiral of the stairs with a dizzy sense of climbing up inside myself as well as outside. I thought I might fall, on the brief landing that led to the door, which was ajar.

Hélène was there, but standing back in the shadows, as if to see without being seen.

"It's you."

She was dressed to go out in what looked like a camel-hair coat, sandy-coloured. Her face for a moment hard to recognize without the old, elaborate make-up, and her hair pulled back under a headscarf.

"Would you like to come in?"

No lights on. Her face haggard under the scarf.

"I'm sorry," I said. "You were going out. I'll come back another time."

I couldn't see her eyes, those backlit eyes, in the darkness of the corridor.

"I was passing through the town," I said. "I'll come back another time."

She made no answering sign. We stood there in silence and I wanted to say I'm sorry for your loss but couldn't begin to form the words, or speak at all.

Then she turned and walked towards the sitting room.

"A cup of tea?"

I shook my head, and followed, and when she turned to look at me for an answer I could only shake my head again, with my throat so full of tears I couldn't trust my voice.

She sat, and although she made no gesture, I sat too, across from her.

Were we going to find some pleasantries? It seemed not. But could we simply sit here forever?

With the light from the window now peering past the headscarf and profiling her features, I could see how deeply lined they were. No more elaborate make-up, no more disguises. She was studying me dispassionately, as if from a great distance.

"Did you have anything to do with his death?" she said at last.

For a moment I was so shocked by the simple clarity of her question that I wasn't sure I knew what she was talking about. My lying, crazy self lay on me as thick as a bearskin. Finally I nodded.

"He was innocent," she said without a pause. She hadn't registering the least surprise at my response. "Completely innocent," she repeated.

"I know," I said. "We were misinformed."

Misinformed. The word came from me unplanned.

It was a mistake, I added, *un malentendu*. A word even more cruelly apt. We had mis-heard.

"You come officially to tell me this?"

I shook my head. "Not officially."

She studied me some more, as if in a new light. Not officially, had I said? Who was I impersonating now?

"There will be some compensation?"

"It's not up to me, I'm afraid."

Go on, I thought, do some more lying. Tell her there'll be a cheque in the mail.

"I have no more connection with government," I said. "Or military."

We sat in further, darkening silence, as if our armchairs were receding from each other.

"What do you do now?"

"I'm in business," I said. "Selling women's clothing."

"Women's clothing," she repeated, dully. I might as well have said I was selling parrots from Madagascar.

"You were about to go out," I said, unable to stand the distance between us any longer.

She nodded. "I'm expected. *On m'attend*. People have been good to me. In a larger place, in Paris, who knows? It would all have been forgotten by now, don't you think?"

She seemed a little more animated. Sorry, perhaps, in some nostalgic or forgiving part of her soul——yet how dare I even think this?——to be letting me go.

"Are you staying with your Garçonnier relatives? I understand the old man is dead."

I nodded again, eluding the first question.

"I'm only here today," I said. "I came to see you."

"I'd better go," she said, almost without a pause.

She rose heavily, and we went to the door.

"I'm sorry." I finally managed. "*Désolé*. I'm so very sorry."

"Do you understand what a good man he was?"

I nodded.

"That's good," she said vaguely. "This new mayor is a good man too. There was even talk of putting up a statue to Olivier." Her voice went hard, to keep out tears. "The Unknown Victim."

After locking the door behind us, she turned back to me in the shadowy stairwell.

"Please don't come back."

Ne revenez pas, je vous en prie .

IT'S SOMETIMES SEEMED to me as if my life ended right there.

Hélène, I don't know what else I could have done, in '43——I mean, of course there are things I could have done, if I'd been clearer in my mind, if I'd been older, wiser, less in thrall to the game of war. I could have refused to complete my mission, refused to kill ODG and aborted the mission, gone home and got canned and waited for history to validate me. I'd have got no mention for this in *Heroes and Heroines of F Section*; well, maybe a paragraph for the Tarn-et-Garonne; but at least Olivier would still be alive and your life wouldn't be ash and I wouldn't have killed an innocent man. Also an exceptionally fine one, as it appears.

I could have done that. I could have aborted the mission. As a result Solange too would have survived, in all likelihood, and her descendents too.

All the factors that blinded me, including obedience and a sordid delusion of heroism, I can see them clear as day now. I can see the young man that I was and I can see why I was blinded. But I've never sought to excuse myself for diving into my adventure with you, even though you wanted it and you started it and Olivier, please God, never knew about it. And even though it wound up meaning even more to me, I think, than it did to you.

The fact that it was so brief is no part of an excuse, it's part of my punishment.

I've never stopped speaking to you in my head, regardless of whether you're still alive or have passed away. At each stage I've needed you to understand. I've needed you to know that it took me eight years to even begin to grasp any of this. And another 20-odd years of my chequered existence before I turned and faced it.

WHEN I GOT back to London I was still so shaky that I took an extra week off work, aiming to pull myself together.

People had surely lived through worse, I kept reminding myself. What was the matter with me?

I was a man who'd been sent to France, by his government, to kill a man, a traitor. In France I had made contact with the target and begun to wonder whether he was in fact the traitor. To make thing worse I had begun an affair with his wife. Despite my doubts I had completed the job and killed the man, only to discover after the war that he had not been the traitor after all, just as I'd feared.

Tough shit.

I was a man who, owing to a clerical error, had killed an innocent civilian in the line of duty.

Get over it. You're not the first.

I was a man who'd been sent to France, by his government, to kill a man who might have been his father. No, that was barmy. Who *could* have been his father, as could many others. I was a man who'd slept with this man's wife, and then killed him.

That was the indigestible part. Or rather it was worse than indigestible. For the crazy space of two breathless weeks I had loved her deeply and obsessively and left in her a part of myself, perhaps the deepest part I had ever opened to the light. So it seemed. Left it in her and in her town and in the fields around it, which I still walked in my dreams. And this whole cock-up left me with no-one anywhere to take it out on.

On arrival in France this time I'd felt horribly moved, immediately, as soon as I smelled the place, moved less by guilt and shame than by a sense of attachment. It was as if by pretending to be a Garçonnier for the 'Anita' mission I had managed to fool myself, as well as others, that the district really contained my family acres. It felt like coming home. Of course France had been my first home, growing up, and I couldn't resist a sense of re-discovery——mine after all! Mine since the Montmartre of my childhood. But that wasn't it. The town itself called to me, this town, not France in general. My heart beat faster as on the way to the *Mairie* I entered the arena of the market square, its surface very faintly mounded towards the ancient paved rectangle at the centre, where the auction ring had stood, that Saturday. My auction ring. The ring where I had saved a life, only to take it again two weeks later. No need to look around for landmarks or check street names, because it was my feet, not my eyes and head, that led me from the *Paradis des Jeunes* to Hélène's door, like a sleepwalker. I had rung the bell, this time, like a trembling child, afraid she wouldn't be there, afraid that she would be. Afraid that she'd look like an old bag, because if she'd aged as much as I had in the in the past eight years she'd look every day of her sixty-odd years. Afraid that she wouldn't have aged a bit and that I'd have to tell her to her voluptuous face, every contour a reminder, that I was the one who'd killed her husband.

So instead of going back to Farjeon and Nephew, Haberdashers, the Monday after my return to London, I took a train to the south coast and booked myself into a bed and breakfast on the seagull-cackling sea front. I didn't really expect to be going back to Farjeon.

Seaside towns have always spelled suicide to me. It's death, not water, that comes lapping at the shaggy green legs of the pier, rusty red underneath the weed and the barnacles. There's nothing morbid about this thought. The sea is a finality, serene, unbroken. You can paddle in its shallows, but no-one walks back alive out of its horrid depths. It's there every morning, the sea, softly booming, tireless despite having lapped away all through the night, like a thirsty dog. It's what awaits. Old people know it, sitting slumped in the sun until the tide comes in with the last summons.

To my eyes everyone on the seafront seemed already dead, from the motionless old folks to the seagulls with their dead eyeballs. They all looked stuffed.

I was ready, I thought each morning, to walk into the sea. Nighttime was the time to do it. Nighttime, imagining I'm on the road to Perpignan, perpetually. Between worlds, hoping never to arrive. This time, just walk into the sea and let it take me home.

Of course there was a part of me that answered back. Come all this way, did you, Runt, to be just another statistic? Another SOE boyo who couldn't hold his water? God knows I was still angry with them, the bastards. Un *malentendu!?* A name mis-heard. A life, two lives, destroyed. Three, now, was it? Feel like handing them another sacrifice, do you?

Nonsense, Major Rawlinson. Pack it in your kitbag and move on. I'm not going to wind up a walking corpse like you, I told the seagulls, squawking and flapping in imitation of life. You're dead. I'm moving on.

Then one morning I woke and found I couldn't move at all.

I couldn't move my arms or legs. I was awake and yet asleep. I couldn't move my lips to speak or cry out. Only my eyes worked, and I could feel tears on my cheeks.

I'll lie in, I thought. I've earned it.

I lay all day. No movement. All I could do was cry. Voices around me, talking about strange behaviour, in recent weeks, on the front and on the pier. Mine, apparently.

The Major's strange behaviour. Accosting people. Chasing seagulls. Shouting. Pointing across to France and shouting.

War hero he's a Major
What's he saying?
Are you sure he's a real Major?
Call the doctor
He's too young to be a Major
He's not young
He can hear you
He can't hear me
He's crying
Call the doctor will you
Look at him he can't hear me poor old sod.

I'd thought I was a submarine, I wanted to tell them, with watertight compartments, but I was wrong.

17. *Demi-mondes*

I'VE NEVER UNDERSTOOD WHERE THE next few years went. That's to say, I know I was in hospital and out of my brain on what the doctors said was a history of far too much drink but I knew it had nothing to do with drinking at all. There should be memories, at least of the doctors and the people on my ward, and there aren't, they've gone. Edie says she never entirely gave up coming to see me, although according to her I barely recognised her and had to have it explained to me on each occasion that this was my mother. She says I talked a great deal but that she could follow very little of it. I think that was the problem, that I had no-one to talk to who could understand anything I said, so I wound up talking to myself to keep everything and everyone out.

In the end it was 'Lucky' Lecky Thurgo, of all unlikely people, my eminent old SOE colleague, whom I have to thank for what passes as my sanity. Lecky, whose career as an undercover agent had been as glorious as mine had been patchy, had gone on to a successful public career as a Member of Parliament with an exaggeratedly large moustache (unlike my own little trademark brush moustache). As soon as the war ended and I traipsed off to Hamburg to join the other malingerers and miscreants in uniform, Lecky had stood for Parliament in his native Cornwall. He stood as a Conservative, and somehow got elected when so many of his party, Churchill included, got booted out. As a result he was one of the stars of the little Tory rump, with his war record——he had a DSO and bar,

I think, to add to his DFC, and the MC and some French medal as well——to go with all the fuss about him, which included a book, *Lucky To The Last*. Luck of the devil it should have been called, if tales of his ruthlessness were true. Perhaps they were all just envy, because Lecky was extraordinarily good to me. He heard from one of our SOE fraternity that I'd fallen off a cliff, mentally speaking, and apparently he visited me in Dorking, where my hospital was. I've no memory of his visit. Perhaps I didn't recognize him either, which would certainly have spurred him to action, if anything would. He organised a fund to get me out of Dorking and into a private home, and pay for a psycho-therapist called Carmichael, on expert on wartime trauma, to see if I was really past recall.

At any rate I've been told that 'Lucky' Lecky paid for part of this, and organised the rest by a whip-round among SOE survivors, and I was also told not to mention that Lecky had anything to do with it. It's all so long ago now that I imagine I can break silence about his kindness. In any case, perhaps he wasn't so much modest as concerned that he might get called on to help out every old SOE soak with a sob story.

My own theory, since really Lecky Thurgo hardly knew me——I couldn't ever have asked him, in order to confirm my theory——is that Lecky may have known that he truly was one of the lucky ones; he may have known how lucky he was to have got that turbo-charged boost in his life, to have been rocketed into the House of Commons just as the dust was settling on his wartime honours. He may have looked at me and seen what he was spared. That's what I suspect. I've heard that his predecessor in Parliament, the chap who represented Lecky's Cornwall constituency before him, was going to stand again in the 1946 election, but was killed in a freak accident after the official end of hostilities. He was killed, this chap, in what was referred to as 'the last shot of the war,' and lo and behold Cornwall looked around and found it had a glorious new son, a Thurgo glistening with medals, to hold off a popular Labour candidate on a tide of sentimental attachment to the late, unfortunate M.P. And then there he was, Lecky, suddenly triumphant in the bosom of the Tory Party. When he could quite easily, as I'm sure he knew (he was a doughty drinker himself), have been wound up being me, the mumbling Major sitting on his Dorking hospital bed.

My therapist, Carmichael, a dear good man who'd been an interrogator during the war and knew something of what I was babbling and mumbling about (Edie said she thought I was talking in code, but I was probably just using a lot of SOE jargon), did actually listen to me and talk to me until I started answering back. We went around, as he put it, like two people in a nursery hit by a bomb, picking up the toys one by one and finding a place for them. The bomb landed next door, he kept reminding me. Not on my head. It landed next door and shook the bejasus out of me, and knocked all my possessions off their shelves. Now we would go round the room, pick them up one by one, dust them down, since many were discoloured and obscured by the plaster dust of confusion, and find a place for them. We would put them next to each other in the right order, the order of years, and introduce them to each other. We would re-establish their relationship as well as their chronology.

This must sound absurd, and infantile, and of course it was infantile in the sense that Carmichael reconstructed me not as a man but as a child, until I could review my own childhood, entire and re-assembled, which was an act that rendered me into a man again. The process left me a little slow (I know this from my own experience of my mental processes and not only from other people's impatience with me), but quite sound. I never feel I'm going to fall through the net any more.

It would have been a lot better, of course, if I hadn't started drinking again as soon as I got out of the nursing home. I had a pretty good pension——again, I think this was partly Lecky Thurgo's influence, because I don't remember having been so well off before I went back to France and returned and started shouting at seagulls—— and as an old soldier with tales to tell I was able to cadge all the drinks I couldn't pay for myself.

Then who did I run into but the first Albert in my life, the original Albert——Albert Ferris, my Aunt Sara's beau and my own father (as I'd been allowed to believe) until the age of twelve. I met him again in a club in Marylebone, one of the daytime drinking clubs created to get around the law in that era of restriction and austerity. Through a haze of cigarette smoke and gin (or it could have been port and lemon, a favourite of mine at the time) I saw a man who looked uncannily like the hairy ape Ferris, but grown older and even balder. It turned out that he owned the club, and several more, along with a hotel in Bayswater that he'd acquired when he pulled out of the Mon Chat Noir and legged it back to Britain before the Germans arrived. To my greater amazement, he was happy to see me. He wanted to talk about Sara and the old days——he missed France worse than I did, as it turned out——and was prepared to flatter me to death to get me to sit still and listen to his tales. Well, perhaps that's not entirely fair. It's possible he really did remember me with a modicum of fondness, as an "independent-minded little sprog," as he put it. I was a little devil, I reminded him, and he clapped me on the back as if I was a boy again, while telling me what a splendid fellow I'd turned into, the famous Major Alan Rawlinson, DSO (*was* I famous?) whose exploits he'd followed with fatherly pride. He'd even wanted to contact me via Edie just to let me know how proud he was that I'd turned out such a good egg.

At the time, that afternoon, it all seemed like alcohol-fuelled mushiness to me. He kept saying I'd been a fighter but a good sort as a child, always ready to stand up for my Auntie Sara (I had no memory of what he meant by this, but perhaps I took her side in their fights), and more of this guff——how he'd liked to think he'd given me something to test myself against, a rough tough Dad to battle and perhaps to hate at times, but to grow up a lot like in the end. Even three sheets to the wind and drunk on nostalgia I couldn't see that I'd grown up remotely like this sleazy, overweight orang-utan on a bar stool, but I tried to give him the benefit of the doubt. He was a convivial fellow, albeit drenched in too much perfume. (Had that been the smell I detested as a child, or was this the stink he used to try and drown his own natural stink? I never discovered.) And he kept buying me drinks. Perhaps, I decided, he hadn't been as bad a surrogate father as I remembered, rowdy, foul-mouthed and quick to cuff myself or Sara with his hairy hand. It was still there, the hairy hand, but the hair was grey now, and when he rested it palm down on the bar it still looked as if a tarantula had crawled out of his shirtcuff and settled on the back of his hand. Only now it was a rather limp grey tarantula, an elderly tarantula. By my boozy calculations, which I kept starting during our conversation and then losing track of and starting again, he had to be 68 now, if he was a day.

We certainly made a rowdy pair, that afternoon, laughing and even doing a drunken dance step or two as we recalled and evoked the glory days of Mon Chat Noir. I saw a few quiet drinkers who were only restrained from intervening by wiser heads, who informed them that one of these two clowns, the big old fat one, was the owner. Another thing that I think we both enjoyed, that afternoon, and which bound us together, was the language we roared and sang. Not many people, in those days, were awash in longing for France. We may have been the only two people in London singing *La Vie en Rose* with such unbridled gusto. There was nothing fake about it either. He really did miss Paris. I did too.

I thought it would be one of those drinking afternoons that, when you met an old SOE pal, became a drinking evening and then became a drinking blank until you woke up in a place you'd never seen in your life, which turned out to be the pal's spare bedroom in the middle of the next day, ready to step out together for a hair of the dog. If you'd asked me while we were drinking and roaring and singing whether I thought I'd never see Albert, the Albert Premier of my existence, again after that day or possibly the next, I'd've said, not a chance.

But he was nothing if not a calculating bugger, Albert Ferris. Mixed in with the sentimental embraces and the lies about how he'd followed my wartime career——Edie might have told him I was in the SOE, but that must have been all of it, surely, unless she later boasted that I was a Major, too——was a sober eye for the main chance. He needed a factotum, he said, an adjutant, an aide-de-camp to help him run his empire. (When he saw that I wasn't exactly leaping off my barstool at the opportunity, it must have occurred to him that from Major to adjutant was a bit of a step down, and he switched my hypothetical role to commanding officer of the occupying Ferris forces.) He was getting old, he said. Too old to keep running around his pubs and clubs (he had a pub, too, a proper pub in

Battersea) to make sure they were running smoothly. He'd been managing these joints for years, and he was knackered and fed up with doing it and he needed younger blood, someone with the energy and the authority to keep and eye on both the customers and the Ferris employees. He was rather cogent when he explained all this——we'd been boozing and singing and recalling the old days for at least five hours, maybe more——and despite his protestations about getting old, which were well attested by the limp grey tarantulas at his collar as well as his cuffs, I was struck by how well he still held his drink. Montmartre, he explained when I complimented his stamina. Pigalle. If you can't hold your liquor after a lifetime of *pastis*, what kind of man are you?

What he wanted was a bully——not a bouncer type, he had plenty of those——but someone who would crack the whip and bring the Ferris word from on high, when club rowdiness was getting out of hand, or a bartender might be salting away too many bottles for himself. Someone who *was* a Ferris, as he put it. Not someone who merely represented Ferris Rex, the imperial baldy, but a Ferris if not by blood at least by upbringing. And wasn't I that Ferris? (I had been, in the truth be told——I'd been Alain Ferris in Montmartre, as a child.) Better still I was a Rawlinson in my own right, a Major Rawlinson, DSO and daytime drinking bar. He'd give me a whacking good salary, he said. I'd have the run of the booze, *ça va sans dire*. Free drink. (I think he saw that register in my glazed eyes like a jackpot on a fruit machine.) And there were the girls. Where Albert Ferris was, girls were never far behind. The Bayswater hotel, which would be under my command, too, as Albert's "right ball," his other term for my role, was party heaven, after hours, and any guest who didn't like the rumpus could clear out, when and if someone could be found to sign him or her out. In practice, Albert said, the people who stayed in the hotel knew what they were taking on, and the presence of classy tarts (classy only, he insisted, none of your Soho trollops) bringing customers along the corridors was the very opposite of a rude shock. It was what they'd come for.

How would I like to be overlord, overseer, right ball and number two, in this country within a country, this oasis, or set of taxi-linked oases, these Ferris-owned revellers' refuges from the cold hypocrisies of British life? A little France in England, as Albert put it, winningly.

I knew perfectly well I'd fallen into the butter. But I played hard to get, negotiated for a share of the bar profits and generally tried to show I wasn't as much of a pushover as the real France had been when the Germans arrived. Albert must have suspected I was a lush. I held my drink pretty well, but few of the drinking club regulars were there because they liked the taste of the stuff. They were there getting systematically blotto for whatever reason, too much to forget, or a lost Eden to remember or just something in the blood than ran them down to the river of booze like a parched mare. So he knew he might be taking on a liability. But we were all liabilities in that world, that *demi-monde* as Albert loved to call it, as if by giving it a French name it transformed the morning-after stench of vomit and the sticky feel of kummel on the door handle into a song by Jacques Brel. We were all liabilities, drunks and cheats who were tender-hearted drinking companions until the wind turned and one wrong word or look and next thing we were rolling on the floor in broken glass trying to head-butt each other. I had no problem with that, and I think Albert must have guessed as much.

As long as I was a loyal liability, I was just what he needed, to let him pass quietly into semi-retirement. What he was tired of wasn't so much doing the rounds, accompanied in a booze-soaked taxi by the resident trollop *du jour*, or *soir*, it was the fights, the needling, the laying down of the law. One look at me, still in my early forties and in good shape recently enough (if he'd looked harder he'd have seen what ten years of drinking had done to me, but I still looked enough like an ex-soldier to fool him), and he saw a man who could use his experience in unarmed combat if required. All it needed, he whispered hotly in my ear, was a couple of those Jap moves, in public, on a large obstreporous customer who wouldn't leave, and word would swiftly get around among Ferris employees. They were the ones you had to keep your eye on.

And he wanted an heir. He wanted to retire gradually to the country, where he already had a small country mansion well-stocked with bottles and trollops *du jour*, near Colchester. Major Rawlinson was an Essex lad himself, Albert Premier pointed out, reminding me of Edie and Sara's Basildon origins. I was welcome any weekend. We'd pop down to Mersea, to the boat (he made it sound like a yacht but it was a modest, rather smelly craft with a huge outboard motor). Who was he going to leave this carefully built-up commonwealth to, unless to his boy, his little Alain, the child of his heart if not, alas, of his loins?

Something in me, surely, saw the last of my self-respect floating gently away on the flood, bobbing away into the mist like some antique bureau. At the same time it made so utterly much sense. It was a comfortable, well-paid niche, hand-crafted for me by Destiny. Granted that it was a world in which I'd always be known as the 'Major' rather than as the Major, a world of frauds and cheats in which no real Major would ever need to lodge. But so much the better. So much the more fun precisely to be the real thing in a world of lies and delusions and charades. Let everyone else be an alias, I'd be my own alias, my party costume would be real self, my uniform real and not rented. And wasn't everything in this job exactly what I'd always yearned for? Disguise, a good lashing of power, violence now and then, free liquor and trollops on demand. Whatever the bobbing bureau was carrying away into the mist, how could it match dominion over the land of Ferris?

As for self-respect, when had I ever located in myself a self with higher aspirations? In Montmartre, hardly. At Merchant Taylors? The real me had been stealing cash. In the SOE? A school for villains. The bit of me that felt——I daren't call it shame, but disappointment, at any rate: that bit was all about things I hadn't done, not things I had. About an Alan Rawlinson I'd never been. Or had failed to be. The Alan Rawlinson who now lifted his glass to toast his future with King Albert was as true to the inner Rawlinson as any version of myself could hope to be, I assured myself. Never mind the Runt who couldn't get Héléne and Olivier du Greffand off his conscience, or Solange Bourget.

But that Runt was still there, and you couldn't swill his body out to sea, not on a river of gin.

IFS. IF ALBERT had lived a little longer. (Which of us was to know he was at death's door when we'd met up again in the drinking club and he signed me up as his second-in-command? Perhaps Albert did know, and was hiding it, from me and from himself. Just as possibly, perhaps he didn't.) If if if. *If* he'd bloody well got round to adjusting his will.

I've never been sure what it argued, exactly, the fact that Albert failed to get me properly installed in his will. I like to think that he just couldn't face dealing with it, like so many people, because it reminded him of his mortality, and that he had no idea his heart was so clogged up he might drop dead at any minute. He reckoned he had plenty of time in which to deal with his will. But I can't help thinking he wasn't quite as fond of me as he pretended. And that the thought of people fighting over his funny, tatty little empire when he was gone didn't entirely displease him.

The stupid bugger had made a will ten years earlier when the resident trollop, Carol, had such a hold on his dick that when she refused him any he further favours until he made a will in her favour, the silly fool gave in. And when he did drop dead on the carpet at the Mon Chat Blanc, as he'd coyly named the Marylebone drinking hole, five, nearly six years after handing me the keys to the palace, Carol Hodgkinson was still his heir. Albert hadn't even seen Carol for close to fifteen years. For that matter nobody in the late emperor's immediate circle knew if Carol was alive or where she was, or how to find out. But in the dear old *demi-monde* there's always somebody who knows where someone else is, even if they're half dead in a cottage in Wales with no electricity or more likely soused in a basement in Worthing. And when there's money up for grabs, you can raise the dead and get them to stake their claim within 48 hours, never mind track down a retired tart to Darlington, where Carol was looking after her ailing Mum. Give her credit, Carol, she wasn't a bad sort. But she had bad memories of Albert, and no love lost for any of his pals.

I worked hard to get the blowsy old love to like me (I'll be honest, she reminded me a little of Aunt Sara), or at least to put up with me, and to try to prove to her that her inheritance was worth most to her if I went on running it as it was and paid her an annual income worth a queen's ransom (in Darlington, anyway). Her advisors, as she kept calling them, her advisors being chiefly her old baggage of a mother, told her to sell the lot, the pub and the clubs and the Flamingo Rose, the hotel (no-one could say Albert had an original or inventive feel for names), and use the money to buy the biggest house in Darlington, where she could entertain——or refuse to entertain——the snobs of Darlington high society who had always regarded her as riffraff and believed the story that she'd been a Soho streetwalker. As she had been.

I kept these dreams of Carol's, her fantasies of provincial revenge, at bay for another few years, but the truth was that without Albert I was finding the old Roman empire a bit of strain to run, myself. I needed a factotum of my own, to deal with the daily crisis, whatever it was, from a disgruntled policeman to a blocked drain. And I was drinking too much, far too much. More than ever before, now that I didn't have to pay for a single drop. The Runt that I insisted wasn't there, the Runt who wished he hadn't done certain things, required daily payment, just as the drains and the police and Carol Hodgkinson did. And that Runt took it in booze.

My belief in my mental toughness had been punctured forever when I had my breakdown in the 'Fifties, after I'd seen Hélène and France again. As far as mind and spirit went, I wasn't a submarine with watertight compartments, despite my boasts. Now it was my body's turn to radio in similar news. I wasn't watertight there either. Like everyone who thinks they can go on boozing into all eternity, I hadn't paid much attention to my shaky feet, my shaking hands, or the face in the mirror. My collapse was diabetic, and after they found me in a room in the

Flamingo where I'd been lying comatose, alone and close to death for three days, I barely surfaced from it at all.

I did, though. I was still the Runt, and a survivor. I did it with the help of Harry and Edie, who were neither of them in their first flush of youth now, and I did it with the help of Harry Junior, an obnoxiously pleasant young fellow who now ran Daddy's furniture emporia while Daddy and Edie spent most of their time sunning themselves in Portugal. But survival can be a mixed blessing, I found. I returned to the London scene a slightly frail and wizened man in his 50s without a job or a sou to my name. Carol had sold up. My old friends and enemies in the *demi-monde* were either amused or sorry to see me a diminished version of myself, but they had no use for me now except as another drinking companion, which was precisely what I was no longer equipped to be.

The one good thing about it all, as Harry put it, was that I couldn't go on boozing or even hanging around pubs unless I wanted to kill myself directly. This wasn't much comfort. But he was right.

Harry let me move into what he and Edie laughingly called the granny flat above the garage of their house in the Algarve. Laughingly and somewhat cruelly, because I'd managed to go almost overnight, or so it seemed to me, from a rough-and-tumble ex-soldier with a drinking problem, like countless others, to a prematurely wobbly invalid who acted as his mother and stepfather's house-sitter and caretaker in the sun.

But I didn't want to go back to the clubs and pubs in the state I was in, and gradually I ceased to miss the Mon Chats, whether Noir or Blanc, and the Flamingo Rose, where I'd lorded it for a while, and resigned myself to a steady, frugal life, living in memories.

I met Jean there, whose husband had been a pilot in the Fleet Air Arm and died in combat in 1943. She had a real granny flat, since she'd been serving as granny to her daughter's children until they finally went off to boarding school in Britain and her arthritis made the prospect of returning to Hereford, where her family lived, rather less attractive than the sunshine of the Algarve.

How persistent the threads of our life are, in the weave! We prefer to think nobody's watching us from on high, as we go about our little rampage. (My arse! Teapot would say emphatically, and brew me another cuppa.) Yet why on earth should Providence pay so much attention to the tiny motifs of our little lives, considering how insignificant they are in the greater symphony of existence? I say this because oddly it was cloth, and sewing, and dressmaking, my old secret passion that kept recurring at odd, untimely moments in my life, which brought us together. As I say, it's always been untimely before; but now at last there was time for it. Edie had asked me to find someone locally to repair a coat that Harry had given her long before the war, and to which she was still attached. In the newspaper I found an advertisement with a name that might have been French and male, Jean, or English and (more likely) female, and I plumped for it.

Jean has been a seamstress all her life. It's a passion and not just a trade, to her. That was how we met and also, in time, how I learned to re-apply my shaking hands to the smoothing out of cloth as I feed it into the clicking, feeding, sewing machine needle, pecking at the material like a tirelessly hungry bird, a sight and sound of which I never tire.

It's the cloth that smooths and soothes my hands, I often reflect, not the other way around.

Most lives are odd, I think, especially mine. I was designed by nature to be a haberdasher, a clothesmaker, a seamster if there is such a word. A dressmaker. Instead I ended up an undercover military daredevil and, if you'll pardon the phrase, an upper middle-class ponce. But at least I managed to wind up with a seamstress as a partner in the end. Jean never wanted to re-marry, and has remained devoted to the memory of her husband, who by one of those quirks of life was also called Alan. Young Harry still likes to tease me about this, saying that at least I'm in no danger of being called the wrong name in a moment of inadvertent passion. Jean's Alan, 'her old Alan,' as he grew to be called in order to differentiate her 'new Alan,' had clearly been a sterling fellow. Or that's how she remembers him, anyway. He may have been lucky (although mind you I wouldn't dare say this to Jean) to have died a sterling fellow, without having his currency tested by the vicissitudes of life——he died at 23. Or he might have come up trumps forever. He was probably that sort of person, as Jean is, a straight arrow. She doesn't like to hear about the Mon Chats, let alone orgies at the Flamingo. I let those old days go, Teapot; did so happily, in exchange for Jean's understanding, where more painful sections of my life are concerned. Jean's devotion to her own memories has made it easier for her to understand my preoccupation with mine, and my need to address them.

WHEN I CAME back again at last to France it was ten months before the 50th anniversary of the Normandy landings, and all the shenanigans that accompanied it. There was no need for shenanigans to celebrate the 50th anniversary of 'Anita,' that classic cock-up. No-one else remembered it, thank God. I came with Jean, my companion of 26 years. Most of the people I knew in and around the town are dead, we learned, including Hélène and even the nice young mayor, Lucien.

I brought Jean out to Labaronnerie, where a youthful Garçonnier with a huge shock of hair, presumably one of old Albert's grandsons, allowed us to stroll through the fields down to the old mill. He had no idea why we would want to go there, and I certainly couldn't tell him, although I explained that I'd been there during the war. He looked understandably puzzled but let us proceed, and use the glorious day to walk with slow care——we are both on the verge of 80——to the pasture land and down to the mill. Along the way, Jean picked a wild rose from the hedge, wrestling with it and twisting it until she got it free, and she handed it to me so that I could place it beside the millrace.

There were so many like Solange, roses cut down before their time, and nothing left for those of us to do who had a hand in that shameful scourge but to cut one last one in her honour.

Once more I wonder if I have the right to make such a gesture, let alone speak. The bloom Jean found must speak for me, small and delicate, a slightly grayish pink, and so open——where in another flower the throat might offer claustrophobic passage sits instead a golden landing pad for visiting bees. It's a rose as fresh and young as Solange was, and always will be. Seeing my own hand, so withered now, bending with it towards the cracked cement, is strange in itself. Why *my* hand? Those who are chosen to survive are rarely the deserving ones, and this, in turn, makes it hard to believe that there's any justice in the world. But if there's no justice there are still warnings; plenty of warnings, and no excuse, it seems to me as I gaze at the sweet pastureland around the millrace, alive once more with immemorial *pissenlits* and thistles, for bringing down the sad colours of war. This was the hell we grew to manhood in, my generation, and which lodged forever in my heart.

It's never Thor who rules, or Mars or whatever Cyclops or cruel Titan you might think that war sets on the throne. It's merely Chaos. For every life cut short by well-directed spite, a hundred are taken by confusion. A thousand, even. All we do in war is accelerate the random. Perhaps that's what we love about it, that we get to turn the page, to peer behind the curtain at the harassed fates working away, faster than usual, with their scissors and thread.

But it will come anyway, whatever it is that they decree, sooner or later. Why hurry fate?

I was about to release the rose onto the cement when I gave it a last look. Its very freshness made me sense how swiftly its charms would fade as it sat there on the chipped stone, losing its lustre in the sun and rain, or blown perhaps into the millrace where at least it would float in its glory for a little moment. That would be better. I straightened up with it and let its curving shape fall to the still, glistening water enamelled with pondweed. Exquisite, the rose lay there on the densely crammed expanse of apple-green florets like something out of heraldry, a lover's devise.

Roy Gumpel

about the author:

Born in the London Clinic as the bombs rained down during the Blitz, Carey Harrison was brought to Los Angeles at the age of one by his actor parents, Rex Harrison and Lilli Palmer. He attended the Lycée Français in New York and Cambridge University in the UK. His prize-winning ouput has been published, performed and broadcast in 34 countries, and includes 12 novels and over 200 scripts and plays for the stage, radio, TV and film. Since 1996 he has been Professor of English at the City University of New York. He is a former activist for the African National Congress and recipient of the Friends of Oliver Tambo award; a former Fellow at the *Wissenschaftskolleg*, the Berlin Institute for Advanced Research; and a member of the Board of the Einstein Forum, an interdisciplinary think-tank in Potsdam, Germany. With his wife, the artist Claire Lambe, he lives in upstate New York.

Author's note: this one is a favourite of my heart. From the moment when Runt Rawlinson first encounters Dr. Olivier du Greffand I felt at home in this twisting tale. How many assassins must have wondered whether they had the right man? As chance would have it, I was once asked——forty years ago and more——if I would be willing to undertake an assassination, for an excellent cause. I declined. In its ownway, this novel revisits that hour of my life, and that decision.

To the memory of my beloved mentor, the distinguished Brazilian educator, Dr. Emanuel Cicero, born in 1907 in Ubatuba, São Paulo. Rector of the College of Rio Grande do Sul from 1943 to 1978, he died in 1988 in Lisbon.

—Maximiliano Reyes, publisher

-FIM-

DR. CICERO BOOKS

www.ingramcontent.com/pod-product-compliance
Lightning Source LLC
Chambersburg PA
CBHW022047240626
47154CB00007B/2602